MW00425123

This book is dedicated to my mother who has always encouraged me to follow my dreams.

Thank you mom, I love you eternally. I finally did it.

Thank God for giving me this ability.

I'd like to acknowledge the following people who have been sounding boards, beta readers, and encouragers when I felt like giving up. They've heard this story told repeatedly yet continued to smile and nod as if it were the first time.

Max, Karla, Peggy, Tina, Cindy, Gerry, Lisa, Cherie, Penny, Pam, Michele, Jude and too many more to name. You all know who you are and you know I love you.

Thanks to all of my coworkers who provided demographic assistance in ways they don't even know.

Thanks to Joshua Robinson for taking my idea for an illustration and turning it into a spectacular cover for this book. You rocked it man.

Thanks to Yowza Design for helping put this project together.

Thanks to David Normand for taking the headshot photo. Your time and expertise are greatly appreciated.

Special thanks to all of my family and friends for purchasing this book and helping me live my dream.

If you bought my book I offer a very special thank you to you as well and I hope this book provides some entertainment and brings you back to read the next case of Mace Dugan.

Chapter 1

Chicago

As he stepped out into the night, a bitter north wind sliced straight through his olive, down-filled jacket cutting all the way to his bones. He pulled up the collar trying to cover as much of his exposed chin as possible as he scanned the area for movement. Across the street from the small restaurant, a flashing sign blinked a temperature of 11 degrees. Halos appeared around the letters in the business names on the buildings. The snow was falling steadily now, painting the ground a brighter white as the flakes accumulated. But, hey, what should one expect of Chicago in mid-winter? He'd never liked this kind of cold, but when you're tracking a bail jumper, you don't have a choice. You go where the trail leads you. Mace Dugan was his name, and he was a bounty hunter for hire. Twenty-two years in this profession had hardened his resolve. Traipsing after his current jumper for ten months straight still had not altered that fact.

Donald Roy Perkins had fled the courtroom of the honorable judge Margaret, Maggie "set the voltage high and let 'em fry" Winston, a feat not easily accomplished on her watch. Cases brought before her tended to follow a strict pattern of arraignment, trial, and sentencing, followed by many years of incarceration. The only child of a career marine, Maggie's whole life to this point had been painstakingly structured. Her father tolerated nothing less than excellence, and that attitude permeated her legal career and personal life. As much as she enjoyed being disciplined in her approach to everything in her life, her code had cost her countless relationships and opportunities for personal happiness.

Suspecting he was about to be found guilty and not willing to risk a possible death penalty verdict, Donald Roy Perkins had jumped his bail. An opened door near the conference room had provided him an opportunity for escape, and he bolted through it into the alley. Breathing heavily, his heart pounding inside his chest, he looked both ways assuring the coast was clear. After pausing on the stoop for a moment, he turned and dashed to his right, constantly checking over his shoulder for a pursuer. He moved past a silver Toyota Prius, then past a beige Ford sedan of some sort and a white Dodge van before finding an unlocked blue Honda Accord. He opened the door, slid inside, lowered the sun visor and caught the falling keys just as the note he'd been given earlier that morning promised. He started the car and was on his way, leaving his lawyer, Joshua Barton, III, to wonder what had happened to his client.

Mace's office phone rang shortly after the realization that Donald Roy Perkins had become a fugitive. The squeaky, frenetic voice of Joshua was almost intolerable for Tonya, Mace's secretary. In her most professional voice, she answered, "Yes, sir. Calm down, sir. I'm having difficulty understanding you. You say you've got a case for Mr. Dugan? Yes, sir. I'll get him the message immediately. Thank you, sir. Goodbye."

Almost a year had passed since the fourth generation defense lawyer with the sparkling acquittal record had returned to the law firm of Caston, White, and Brockhoeft to explain the whole mess to the "old man" himself, Mr. Caston. Recurring nightmares of that day haunted Joshua almost nightly. Ghostly figures taunted his sleep repeating his words from that Tuesday morning, "Donald Roy Perkins is gone. Donald Roy Perkins is gone." Regardless of the advice he'd received, the echoes of these nightmares never seemed very far away. Sleep eluded Joshua, and the stress was beginning to take its toll on his physical features. Even sleeping pills and multiple glasses of whiskey offered him no solace. Neither hot baths of lavender nor meditation helped any either. Mostly, he lay awake in his bed feeling sorry for himself. He was convinced the whole universe was conspiring against him. A loud vibration followed by the theme for Mission Impossible ring tone startled him. With a cold sweat beading on his forehead, he reached toward his dresser. Seeing the light from his phone dancing on the table, Joshua grabbed the moving target and flipped it open.

Inaudibly, Joshua mouthed hello several times into the microphone.

"Joshua, is that you?" he heard from the receiver. "It's Mace. Are you okay man? I can barely hear you." The phone whistled in Mace's ear as he waited for the reply.

Several seconds passed before Joshua's familiar raspy voice could finally be heard. "Hello, Mace. You woke me from a sound sleep," Joshua lied. "What time is it anyway? Why are you calling me so late?"

"Relax, man. It's only ten thirty your time," Mace replied. "I'm in Chicago freezing my ass off, but I may have a lead. This feisty little redhead named Amiee at Rockit Bar and Grill remembered seeing someone who resembled the photo of our missing man. Apparently he came in several days in a row this week. She recalls him reading a folded newspaper while mumbling on about needing to get to a safe house yesterday afternoon. He always ate alone with his back to the wall and usually had the special of the day she said. That's why she remembered him; he'd ask her for the same table whenever he came by. Once he even refused to eat since his table was occupied by other patrons. That seems like a guy with some military savvy, eh, buddy? Hey, Josh, did you two ever discuss him knowing anyone here during your discovery and interview process?"

"I don't recall him saying anything about knowing anyone in Chicago, Mace. But since I was just awakened, I'd really need to check my notes to be 100 percent certain; you know what I'm saying. Can this wait until I can do some research and buzz you back; or do you need to know immediately? I have to attend a meeting tomorrow with the old man anyway. After that ends, if I still have a job, I'll check and give you a call. OK?" Realizing he could do nothing to help Mace tonight, Josh decided to go back to sleep and call back after his meeting. Mace ended the call and slipped his phone inside his inner coat pocket.

Joshua had amassed a nearly perfect litigation record thus far. He'd been able to gain acquittals for 98 percent of his clients. Moving steadily up the ranks of the firm's junior lawyers, he was preparing for what he thought would certainly be a partnership offer. Instead, now a meeting with the old man, Mr. Caston, the senior partner of the firm, had been scheduled to discuss his future. The way Mr. Caston had said the words "your future" during their phone conversation sounded

foreboding. What if he were informed that he'd just

been fired? He would lose the posh uptown

apartment. The leased Mercedes, along with his

custom made suits and shoes would be gone, also.

Meals he received gratis from Las Vegas restaurants

like his friend Wolfgang Puck's, Planet Hollywood,

Andre's at the Monte Carlo and others would

certainly come to a halt, as well. He needed to get

some kind of information on the whereabouts of

Donald Roy Perkins before that meeting. Perhaps

some good news could appease the desires of Mr.

Caston and stave off his impending termination.

Mace had scanned the phone book for a

business named Safe House in the Chicago area but

found nothing. He dialed the number for information

at the library and asked if they had any knowledge of a business with that name. The friendly voice replied she couldn't find anything matching his request. After hanging up the phone, Mace decided to go upstairs to the bar and begin the age old process of asking questions and divining answers from drunken gibberish.   One good thing about alcohol is that it generally causes the person drinking it to be much less cautious about answering questions. Buy someone a few rounds, and you could gain a new friend for life, along with the answers to almost any questions you might want to ask.

Whenever one is hoping to glean information by buying drinks for unsuspecting bar patrons, one should be sipping a watered down drink that appears alcoholic in nature. Mace knew slipping the bartender a twenty dollar bill would aid him in this illusion. The bartender would fill his glass with water and pocket the nice tip while the new friend would be feeling the effects of the booze. Tonight Mace was getting very little useful information, and since he had been working this tactic for the past couple of hours or more, his butt was going numb. He must've spent a cool 100 bucks while interviewing several bar goers and still he had no idea where this safe house could be. "Someone should alert bar owners that those stools they usually buy aren't much more than a raised slab of granite on a stick," Mace mumbled as he slowly stood and stretched to release some of his stiffness. Needing a cigarette, he decided to step outside to clear his head and formulate his next move.

The trusty Zippo lighter that had been around the world with Mace struggled to stay lit in the stiff night breeze and it died out. Mace closed the top, furiously shook the keepsake side to side coaxing extra butane to the wick. Finally he flipped open the case, struck the flint wheel and shielded the flame. Mace bent his neck to light the tip of the cigarette and he saw it there in the amber glow. Against the side of the building mere inches from his boot, something caught his eye. Without thinking, he bent down and picked up the wet, discarded matchbook. Natural curiosity urged him to open it when he realized it had come from the Bellagio Casino in Las Vegas. "Could this have any connection to my case?" he asked himself. "Why else would something from over 1800 miles away be taunting me here in

Chicago?" Inside the cover he discovered a partial

number. Melted snow had smeared the ink

somewhat, and he couldn't make it out in its

entirety, but there was definitely a name there as

well.

Perhaps if he could figure out the name and

number there, he might get closer to capturing

Donald Roy Perkins. Then Mace would return him to

Las Vegas, collect the reward money, and head off to

a nice warm beach for a well-deserved vacation filled

with tropical drinks and bikini clad beauties. Mace

decided this matchbook held enough information for

him to return to the hotel and work on it. Mace

drove to the Days Inn O'Hare West on East Higgins

Road. As he pulled the rental car into the nearly

empty parking lot, he noticed the eerie tree shadows

along the pavement. They seemed alive and moving, almost reaching for him. Once in the room, he began diligently working to decipher the numbers and what was left of the name on the matchbook. His mind was so tired from lack of sleep and being on constant vigil that he simply couldn't make any progress. He just needed to get some sound sleep and begin fresh tomorrow. Softly he laid his head on the pillow in hopes of sleeping.

Joshua tossed and turned in his bed. Mace's words about the safe house were playing over in his head like a skipping record. Ever since he'd spoken with Mace on the phone, his mind had gone into hyper drive trying to remember the many times he'd spoken with Donald Roy Perkins. Every noise he heard was amplified. Joshua flipped his pillow over, fluffed it, and buried his face in it. Still the sounds

persisted. The clicking of the ceiling fan, the ice

maker's motor refilling the tray, and the wind

whistling outside his window. Doubts began

creeping into his mind. What if he'd hired the wrong

bounty hunter?   He had asked everyone he knew

who they would use if they found themselves in his

predicament. The answer was unanimous. There

was none better than "Mace, the Ace" Dugan. God,

how he hoped they were right. His entire career was

riding on the line here. It was if he was "all in" on a

hand of Texas hold em and someone else was

betting with his money.   Eventually feeling

somewhat reassured that he had hired the best, his

mind relented and Joshua faded into

unconsciousness.

Joshua awoke to the bright morning sun in a clear blue sky. He wondered how this could have happened to him. This was supposed to be a simple case. He was told he would be provided with all the evidence needed to guarantee a not guilty verdict for Donald Roy Perkins. Something went terribly wrong while he was planning his defense though. Not only was he left without any evidence to present, but his promised star witness had never come forward, and his client had disappeared. No wonder he had been guzzling Maalox and sweating through his fresh shirts as soon as he put them on.

The last ten months he'd felt like he was alone in a shrinking room. With every direction he turned, it seemed his options were becoming more and more limited, and his chance for a positive outcome was decreasing.

Even his relationship with Dawn Burns, his on again off again girlfriend, had been suffering. They both used each other as friends with benefits whenever the mood would strike. Lately, Joshua hadn't been able to answer the call. Last night was just another bad attempt to allow the sweet release of sweaty, unabashed sex to divert his mind from this unending search for Donald Roy Perkins. Even when Dawn approached in a soft, sheer black negligee showing her firm, taut stomach and her shapely rounded buttocks while slowly teasing herself and moaning, "Oh, Joshua, I've been a very naughty girl. Don't you want to spank me?" Her long red hair cascaded over her shoulder and she flashed him her best "come hither," as her erect nipples strained against the soft fabric, but all he could think of was that son of a bitch

Donald Roy Perkins. With Joshua's lack of attention and performance, Dawn became upset, threw on her overcoat and stormed out of the apartment. Her parting words, "This is the last time, Joshua Barton….You hear me!" reverberated off the walls. "You'd better get your head screwed on straight if we're to have any future together. I dropped everything in hopes of seeing you finally coming out of this funk you've been in, only to find you're a thousand miles away from me. Don't bother calling me anymore until this case is over. GOOD BYE!" And with that said, she slammed the door behind her.

It was probably just as well that she left since Joshua had to be in the office in two hours anyway. Alone with time to think, he walked over to the picture window that overlooked the Las Vegas skyline. Catching his reflection, he was taken aback by what stared back at him. What had happened to that all-American, clean-cut boy who grew up helping his parents on their ranch? Where was that determined fellow who'd worked so hard to graduate UCLA Law School near the top of his class? His brown eyes that once gleamed with confidence were instead bloodshot and rimmed in dark circles. The normal upright shadow was hunched and haggard from too many sleepless nights and near exhaustion. This vision had a sobering effect. Suddenly welling up inside him was the renewed resolve that had allowed him to leave home a ranch hand and remake himself into something better than anybody ever dreamed. He brushed aside his wavy blonde hair and smiled for the first time in quite a while; time to dress and go face Old Man Caston.

Relaxing on her brown leather couch, shoes scattered on the floor, Maggie wondered just how she'd gotten to this point in her life. She'd graduated first in her class, was the only senior to beat the professor in his mock courtroom, and had an incredible litigation record, which led to her landslide victory when she threw her hat in the ring for judge. The question nagging her now was how at 49 years of age had she become Maggie "set the voltage high and let 'em fry" Winston? Was it her conservative belief that the guilty should actually pay for their crimes? Was it her fault that criminals who saw other judges had very little deterrent from becoming repeat offenders? Should she dole out lesser sentences just to be more popular at the boys club? "Not on your life!" she exclaimed, as she slammed back the bourbon and water. Who cared if she'd been divorced three times? Maggie could always use any of the number of gentlemen escort services in Las Vegas if she had some social function that required her having a date. "It's a tough world, baby, and sometimes bad things happen to good people," she told herself as she poured another drink. "If you could go back in time, would you change anything you've done or accomplished?" she asked herself.

Ignoring the question and waving her hands over her head as if to clear away a smoke cloud, she decided to order Italian from Franco's, her favorite restaurant. Besides, if she had it delivered, she wouldn't be seen eating alone, yet again. Picking up the phone, she dialed the all too familiar number and said, "Hello, Franco's? This is Maggie Winston, for delivery please. Yes, that's the correct address. I'd like to order the veal Marsala with steamed vegetables, a salad with your house Italian dressing, some warm breadsticks, and tiramisu for dessert. Add a bottle of Joseph Phelps Insignia cabernet sauvignon 2002, also." Ever since it had won the Wine Spectator magazine Wine of the Year award, she'd fallen in love with its taste. It was one of her vices, despite its

$225 price tag. What good was all the money she had if she couldn't enjoy her passion for fine wine?

Mace was sound asleep when the front desk rang his room. Still feeling the effects of sleep deprivation, he knocked over the half empty glass of water on the nightstand creating a visibly noticeable wet spot on the carpet as he answered, "Yeah, hello?"

The cheery voice on the other end said, "Good Morning, Mr. Dugan. It's now 9:00 a.m., and this is your wake up call. Would you like a bellhop to help with your luggage?"

"No thanks," Mace replied, "I've got it covered. What's the temperature outside?"

" It's about 21 degrees according to our thermometer" she replied.

"Great. Goodbye."

"Goodbye Mr. Dugan."

Rubbing his tired eyes and straining to bring the room into focus, Mace began to remember the matchbook. Yes, the matchbook. As he was drifting off to sleep after searching Google, he decided that today he would take the short trip from Chicago to Milwaukee and check out a bar called the Safe House. Did he believe that the answers would be found there? He wasn't sure of what he believed any more, but he knew that he must press onward.

After showering and dressing, Mace grabbed his suitcase and was out the door. He quickly loaded the trunk of his BMW, hopped behind the wheel, and headed to the nearest gas station for a fill up and some breakfast. The snowplow had already been through the parking lot, but the snow was accumulating once again. Twenty gallons of premium gas, a large hot cup of coffee and a package of Ding Dongs later, he eased onto the highway looking for Interstate 94. In 84 miles he'd be in Milwaukee heading for 779 North Front Street where he'd meet Linda Wilkes who managed the Safe House Bar. She had agreed to allow him a private viewing of the secret passages and the gathered video footage of the last few days after he'd explained the reasons and flirted with her over the phone.

The drive up I-94 would've been enjoyable if it weren't for the fact that winters in northern Illinois could be brutal. Winding along the lake and enjoying the scenery must surely be a pastime of many residents and visitors during the summer months; however, as Mace rolled along amazed at the icy roads and snow drifts, all he could think of was why Donald Roy Perkins would be so far from his home. Was he missing something? A trick Mace had always used was to try to put himself in the mind of a jumper to figure out what their next move might be and beat them to the spot. So far with Donald Roy Perkins, it had been a futile exercise. Every time he'd formulated a plan of what his next move might be, Mace had been out in left field. Nothing this guy was doing made any sense to him. Instead of seeking out relatives or known acquaintances in Texas or Florida, here he was freezing to death in the northern states. This was one jumper who kept Mace scratching his head. The longest he'd ever taken to track a jumper was a year and three days to date, and this case had him thinking he might be setting a new record.

"Am I beginning to get old and slow?" Mace wondered. He shook his head and pushed those negative thoughts out of his mind as the traffic thickened and slowed due to snow drifts. That kind of defeatist thinking wouldn't help him now. He had to concentrate as visibility worsened to a mere five to ten feet. He knew he'd better keep his eyes on the road and pay attention to his driving or he would end up wrecked or stuck in a snowdrift. Eighty-four miles never seemed so long. With slowing traffic, icy conditions and a few flurries, the trip had taken more than twice the expected time. He may not make his noon appointment with Linda. Now why hadn't he programmed her number into his IPhone?

The deli where they had agreed to meet was practically empty when Linda arrived. She looked around and saw several people getting their orders to go. A young man was reading, and an elderly couple sat at a table holding hands enjoying each other's company. Checking her watch, she noticed that she had already been at McDougal's nearly 45 minutes. Was she going to be stood up? Saturday was her usual day for sleeping in, hitting the gym, having her spa treatment, and finally treating herself to a little shopping with the girlfriends.

Deciding to give Mace an additional fifteen minutes

before leaving, Linda ordered a refill of her latté and

perused the Journal Sentinel for shoe sales. She missed

the companionship of the opposite sex, but since Mace

sounded like such a rugged man over the phone, she

decided to forego the usual Saturday routine to meet him

instead. She had gotten up early, bathed, and chosen her

favorite sexy dress and heels. Leaving her hair down and

loosely curled, she applied light eye shadow, a small

amount of blush, mascara, and red lipstick for that proper

look of sophistication, yet approachability. She placed a

few drops of her favorite perfume behind her ears and

between her breasts. Surely if the real Mace matched her

fantasy of last night, fifteen more minutes couldn't hurt.

Besides, she'd never met a skip tracer before.

There was a parking spot directly in front of McDougal's Deli. Mace pulled his car to a halt and checked himself in the mirror. Maybe, just maybe, this trip wouldn't be a total waste of time. Walking through the front door, he searched the small crowd in the deli for Linda. Wow, could that be her? What a stunner! She had gorgeous light brown hair and a wide smile with perfect red lips. She was wearing a black dress that revealed the slightest hint of cleavage. Her green eyes locked onto his as he stood near the coat rack and shook the fallen snow from his jacket. She stood up as he approached. He deduced that she was probably about five feet, six inches before stepping into her open-toed red stilettos. "Hello, Linda? I'm Mace," he greeted.

"Yes. I'm Linda Wilkes," she answered. "I was just about to give up on you. What happened? You weren't thinking of ditching me, were you?" she teased.

He began to explain the treachery of I-94 as the waitress approached with a warm smile and asked if she could take his order. Mace asked Linda what she had and she told him about her nonfat vanilla latté and cherry scone.

"Sounds good," he said. "Only make mine with regular milk please."

"Sure thing. It'll be right out," the waitress said.

Patting his stomach, he teased Linda that she didn't appear to need nonfat milk in her latte'. He winked and flashed his friendliest smile.

Linda told him that she normally jogged during the summer months, but it was always so cold in the winter that she changed her diet to help keep her shape. They chatted for a little while as they both finished off their orders. Finally, they prepared to trudge outside. The day was becoming increasingly colder and looking like blizzard conditions. The storm Mace had driven through was arriving with its full force. Grabbing their coats from the rack, Linda indicated to Mace that hers was the black Burberry wool and cashmere one. The snow crunched beneath their feet and cars whizzed by as they stood in the stoop waiting for a break to cross the street. The light changed to red, and they made a mad dash to the opposite sidewalk.

Linda reached into her purse and pulled out a large ring of keys at the entrance to the Safe House. Locating an old skeleton key, she slipped it into the lock remarking that she was glad the heat was still on from last night. Entering the room, Mace saw a huge bar, about ninety feet long and lined with the same bar stools he remembered from Chicago the night before. The walls were covered in James Bond movie posters and spy lingo.

In the corner was an old public phone booth next to a sign that read, "Things are not always what they seem."

"That's pretty ominous," Mace thought to himself.

Linda noticed the quizzical expression and asked, "What does that look mean?"

Mace motioned over to the sign and said, "It's almost like it's mocking me."

She grinned and said, "Oh you; it's only a sign on a wall. Come on let's go to the video control room. I need to take these shoes off and warm my feet by a heater. The things we girls do to look good for you guys."

Mace asked Linda if a foot rub would help thaw her feet and she nodded. She slipped into a chair, and Mace removed her shoes and began gently massaging from her toes upward. Linda leaned back almost purring and said, "Oh my God, Mace. You have some very strong hands that are quite talented, too." Realizing she might

be appearing easy, she abruptly pulled her foot from his

grasp and said, "That's good. Thanks. Thanks very much."

Slightly flushed, she sat upright and asked, "You wanted

to check the video against your photo of what's his name

again?"

"Donald Roy Perkins" he said.

"So let me see it, and I'll help you search through

these videos to see if he appears. What did you say he

did again? He looks so nice. He has caring eyes. Seems

like a sweet guy."

"The charges against him allege that he brutally

murdered his family bu stabbing them to death and

jumped bail before being sentenced to life in prison."

"Wow! And you think he was here in my nightclub

last night?"

" Dunno for sure."

He told Linda about the matchbook he had found in Chicago and that he had followed the trail to her bar on a hunch. "It's really almost a shot in the dark though Mace stated flatly. Let's begin searching through these tapes to see if this trip is worth it or just another dead end for me. How many of these did you say there are?" he asked.

"We have fifty cameras installed in strategic locations throughout the bar and each tape is maybe...six hours long," she replied.

"Damn!" he exclaimed. "That's a lot to sift through. Let's get started, and we may as well think about having some lunch delivered. "Do you like Chinese food, Linda? If you know any good restaurants around here,

I'm buying," Mace said. "After all, I owe you at least that much for your help and hospitality, too."

"I love Chinese food, and I'm sure we can find some other way for you to repay me," Linda said with a smile. Mace had secretly hoped that would be her response indicating he was correct, too, in sensing some mutual attraction between them. After all, judging from her shapely figure, he was sure she would be a fantastic lover and had already been so briefly in his mind as he rubbed her feet and listened to her intoxicating voice.

Time seemed to be moving in fast forward as they carefully studied each tape; some were dark and blurry, and others were pointing off to nowhere or tracking shoes of patrons as they passed by. "Humph, not much help, huh?" Linda asked.

"We've been at this for almost three hours, already," he replied realizing it was 4:30, "and not even a hint of useful information."

"Well, not exactly," Linda joked. "I've found ten or so cameras that either need repair, replacement, or refocusing."

"Very funny, Linda."

"Oh come on, Mace. Follow me home, and I'll make you a hot, home cooked meal instead of more take out food."

The littered boxes of half-eaten fried rice, dumplings, and sesame chicken were cold by now. Mace never refused an invitation from a beautiful woman, and this might also allow him to uncover some evidence that Donald Roy Perkins had indeed been there. He agreed to follow Linda home. What's the worst thing that could happen? He could get a nice meal, a hot shower, and quite possibly the favors of a beautiful woman if he played his cards right.

Linda drove a red Mercedes, easily noticed on the nearly empty city streets. Just a short distance from the bar was a well-hidden entrance to an exclusive gated neighborhood. Pulling up to the small white guardhouse surrounded by snow-covered swamp milkweed plants, Linda paused and motioned back towards Mace's car while talking with the security guard. Mace was preparing to stop, but the guard waved him through, smiled, and gave him a thumbs up sign as he passed. Thank goodness, because the wind was freezing as it came in through the car window. The poor man had frost on his mustache and was in an obvious hurry to get back inside the guardhouse. "Well," Mace mumbled, "this just keeps getting better and better." Rounding the curved, tree lined streets with identical mailboxes; they arrived at a mansion mostly hidden from view by shrubs and hedges.

Linda's home had a triple wide circular driveway that split around a grassy area, where stood a sculptured angel in a sparkling snow dress. Icicles dripped from the trees creating a winter wonderland in the front yard. A gazebo and tree-swing were nestled off to one side. Huge, shuttered windows adorned the front of the house. Gaslights marked the front entrance on brick columns while footlights illuminated the walkway under the snow. The garage door rose to expose enough parking for four or five cars. Linda pulled into the first spot and waved Mace into the second. A snowcat vehicle occupied the third spot with the remaining two empty.

"Hey, can you recommend a hotel for me?" Mace asked as he closed the car door behind him. "After dinner I'm gonna need a place to crash for awhile." Linda scoffed and replied, "You can stay here. There's plenty of room, and I even brought the remaining surveillance tapes from the bar. I thought you may want to study them after dinner. What do you say?"

"Oh, yeah, that sounds great," he said. 'I'm certain that the beds here will be much more comfortable than any hotel, and I could really use a good night's sleep."

The garage closed and they entered the house. Linda discarded her high heels near the door and yelled over her shoulder, "Wipe your feet Mace. Why don't you go shower while I prepare dinner?"

"Sure thing," he replied. "That sounds like a plan."

"It's settled then. Come on. I'll give you the nickel tour and you can get cleaned up before we eat."

Coming from the high roller suites of Vegas, Mace thought he'd seen luxury before. When Linda had said earlier that there was plenty of room, he had no idea how right she was. The formal dining room could easily accommodate 20 to 30 guests. An Olympic-sized, indoor heated pool with its own changing room was just to the side of a gourmet kitchen. The workout facility was comprised of a treadmill, a stair stepper, some free weights, a stationary bicycle, and a medicine ball. Mirrors and televisions were placed strategically in the room so one could exercise while being entertained or keeping abreast of the latest news. The rest of the lower level of the home consisted of four rooms complete with their own full baths, a wet bar, and a large fireplace with a stone hearth.

Following Linda up the carpeted stairs, Mace could not take his eyes off her body. "She must spend hours working out," he told himself. So why was she in this big house all by herself? Dying to ask her this and more, he bit his lip and continued climbing. Once upstairs the layout was pretty easy to figure. To the right was a media room with a 55 inch plasma television and projector. They paused here just long enough to drop off the tapes. Next to it was a balcony that allowed for viewing of the downtown skyline and the lights along the waterfront. You could see the stars twinkling and almost hear the droning of the ship's engines as they entered and exited the port. Mace imagined she had spent many a summer night gazing into the darkness and absorbing the breathtaking view. To the right, even further down the hall, were four bedrooms. They returned to the staircase and went left where Linda pointed out the master suite and the final two bedrooms. At the entrance to the master suite they stopped, and she told him he could have either room next to hers; the choice was his. Mace inquired of her which was the quietest. She suggested the room to her left which she lovingly called the "man room." He agreed and she left him there saying she would be in the kitchen if he needed anything and to make himself at home. He thanked her again and entered the room.

It was easy to see why this was called the man room. The walls were decorated with sailboats and sailing paraphernalia. There was a compass, a sextant, and what appeared to be a sheet rope, as well. On a desk to his right lay a maritime bell and some nautical maps of Lake Michigan. One wall was covered with a discarded spinnaker and a paddle for effect. A walk-in closet took up another wall and huge armoire with dressing mirror the other. It suited him just fine. Little did Linda know Mace had served in the navy before being honorably discharged for somnambulism, the medical term for sleep walking.

Throwing his suitcase onto the king-sized bed, he grabbed

his shaving kit and headed for the shower. The steaming

water was just what his tired muscles needed. It had been

quite some time since he'd had a shower this hot, and he

languished in the small luxury. Mace could hardly wait to

test that bed tonight. Hotel mattresses aren't always the

most comfortable. He lathered himself with body wash

and finished his shower. He shaved, dressed in his

favorite muscle shirt and pulled jogging sweats over his

gray boxer briefs. He sat on the bed, slipped his feet into a

pair of Dockers and paused. Standing, he admired himself

in the full- length mirror on the inside of the door. There

he stood, 6'2", powerful tattooed arms, his short dark

hair beginning to gray slightly at the temples. Each of his

tattoos was a reminder of someone special in his life. He

had a heart with the words "Love you Mom" and an

anchor with his father's initials. "Oh yeah, you look good Mace," he told himself. He splashed on some cologne, and then headed for the kitchen.

A delicious aroma greeted him as he descended the staircase. Mace couldn't wait to see what awaited him in the kitchen. Flickering flames from the candles and the clinking of glasses let him know Linda was pouring wine. The glow made her look even more alluring, and he knew at the very moment how much he wanted her. Linda had changed into a black silk kimono and her house slippers. Turning to catch him staring at her she said, "I hope you don't mind. You were taking so long I decided to change into something a little more comfortable."

"No, I don't mind at all. You look lovely."

"Mmm, yes, that will work out nicely," she said after sipping the wine from her glass. "Are you ready to eat?"

"I'm starved, Linda."

"Me too," she chimed.

"What are we having?" Mace questioned.

"Well, since this is your first trip to Milwaukee, I thought I'd offer you some of my grandmother's secret recipe shrimp and corn soup, accompanied by filet mignon, and a nice little sauvignon blanc I found while vacationing in France one summer. If you have a penchant for something sweet, we could split a hot fudge sundae. Sound good to you?"

" Yeah, it sounds perfect," he replied.

"Great!' Linda said enthusiastically. "Now, how would you like your steak? The grill is waiting on us."

"I'll have mine medium, please," he stated.

She nodded, smiled to herself and said, "Just the way I like mine, too. Coming right up, Mace."

The conversation flowed over dinner just as easily as the wine. Mace discovered that Linda's dad had been a shipping magnate before he and his wife were killed when Linda was only nineteen. She had no siblings, so the entire inheritance, including the 10 million dollar life insurance policies, had gone to her. After living the jet set lifestyle for several years, she decided that she preferred managing the Safe House. This proved beneficial for her wellbeing instead of staying home alone because she would easily become bored. Twice before she had been engaged, only to discover the men were merely after her fortune. Instead, now she and her girlfriends would spend time dining, enjoying one another's companionship, and shopping. Her laugh was almost melodic, and Mace found himself becoming mesmerized by the movement of her lips and her lilting voice.

They talked and ate. She opened a third bottle of wine as the conversation continued. Mace shared with her his love of puzzles and travel that he had blended together into a career as a skip tracer/bounty hunter. Suddenly he leaned in and kissed her softly on her lips, still damp from her last sip of wine. Half expecting to have his face slapped, he found instead she pressed into him. They kissed deeper and he soon tasted her tongue inside his mouth. He ran his hand to the back of her neck entangling it in her hair as he pulled her closer to him. When he released his hold on her, she whispered, "Let's go upstairs."

"You're reading my mind, Linda," Mace replied.

"Grab the rest of the bottle," she said, "and I'll get the glasses." Hurriedly they ascended the stairs to her bedroom. She flung open the door and began to grab at Mace's sweats pulling them down to his ankles. He tugged the belt tied around her waist; she rolled her shoulders back and stood before him completely naked. Mace paused to take in her beauty. Pulling her into his arms he quipped, "Oh, you can definitely forget ordering the nonfat latte' tomorrow. We're about to burn off far more calories than that."

Her hair was soft and smelled of vanilla. God had, in his infinite wisdom, given her two of the most perfect breasts he had ever seen. Her hourglass shape was that of a 1950's pinup girl he'd seen in his father's mechanic shop long ago. Her legs were long and toned. Her perfectly tanned body looked as if she had just returned from some exotic summer island. She was truly a vision.

Mace removed his shirt exposing a forty-six inch chest

and flat stomach. "I'm no Charles Atlas, but I do keep

myself in shape," he said.

"So I can see. Now, what else do you have for

me?" she purred as she ripped off his boxers. They spent

time teasing one other before making the most

passionate love either had ever had the joy of

experiencing. They kissed incessantly, and Mace stared

into her eyes as his body pinned her to the mattress in

sweet embraces. He brought her to orgasm several times

before he reached his own. Finally exhausted, they

drifted off to sleep in each other's arms.

"Who cares about Donald Roy Perkins? Not me.

Not any more, tonight," Mace thought.

A bright morning sun greeted him, and he reached for Linda but found she was not in the bed. He called out to her but got no answer. Mace quickly went to his room, showered, brushed his teeth and wiped the sleep from his bloodshot eyes. He cursed when he realized the time. His watch showed noon already, and he was no closer to finding Donald Roy Perkins.

Joshua's meeting with Mr. Caston, the chief partner of the law firm, finally arrived, which was a relief. He didn't know how much more waiting and wondering he could take. He stepped into the outer office and alerted Barbie, Mr. Caston's secretary, of their appointment. Quietly she picked up the phone and said, "Mr. Caston, Joshua Barton is here to see you.

"Have a seat," she said, "Mr. Caston will be with you shortly." Sweat was already seeping into Joshua's under shirt and darkening the arm pits. He could feel that clammy sensation and rapidly rising heartbeat as he sat

and played out the upcoming horror he imagined would

occur as soon as he entered the office. He had chosen his

favorite slate blue suit, a starched white button down

collar shirt, and his infamous red power tie. Whenever he

wore it, he always felt authoritarian. Minutes later,

though it felt like an eternity to Joshua, Barbie

announced, "Mr. Caston will see you now."

Inside the dimly lit, expansive office were leather

chairs and a large conference table with a small lamp in

the center next to a speakerphone. He had heard all

about the size of the old man's office, but this was his first

and quite possibly last time to see it with his own eyes, so

he was slowly drinking it all in. A large oak bookcase filled

with law books covered one entire wall behind the table.

Turning around he saw Mr. Caston motioning him to sit in

a high back, red leather chair in front of his desk. Large

windows allowed a view of the Las Vegas skyline, and in the distance he could make out the airport. A Lady Justice statue complete with blindfold and scales along with a suit of armor were to the left of Mr. Caston's marble topped, custom made mahogany desk. Squaring his shoulders trying to appear more confident then he really felt, Joshua walked over and shook Mr. Caston's hand. Smiling, he said, "Good morning, sir. You asked to see me?"

"Yes, Joshua, I did was Mr. Caston's reply. I've become aware of this Donald Roy Perkins fiasco. What can you tell me about his possible whereabouts and what's being done to apprehend him?"

"Well, Mr. Caston, I've got the best guy in the business tracking him for us. At last report he was in Chicago and had a lead he was following. I'm waiting to hear from him any minute to get another update."

"Very well, Joshua," Mr. Caston said. "You know I've had my eyes on you for some time now, and I'd hate to be disappointed by you. We wouldn't want that now would we, Joshua? I don't deal well with employees who disappoint me," he continued. "In fact, I fire them!

"But I like you, boy. You remind me of myself in my heyday. The pressure is rising on this one, Joshua. Don't let it explode all over you. Do you understand what I'm saying here?"

"Yes, sir, I understand. Mr. Caston. I won't let that happen. You have my word."

"Good, I see we understand each other," he said. "Keep me informed on this, Joshua. Speak to no one else but me directly. You're dismissed."

"Thank you, Mr. Caston. I'll let you know the minute we have something tangible."

"You do that, Joshua. Good bye."

"Good bye, Mr. Caston."

Standing in the elevator loosening his tie, Joshua breathed a sigh of relief. Ok, that could've gone much worse than it did he told himself. It wasn't fun but at least the old man hadn't fired him yet. Now to call Mace and get that damned update. "He'd better have some good news for me or I'll...I'll...," Joshua's voice trailed off as he reached for his cell phone. Exiting the elevator, he hit the voice activation dial and said, "Call Mace." The number began to tone in the phone and soon he heard, "Hey, this is Mace. You know the drill. Leave it after the beep, and I'll call you back later. Out." Beep.

"Mace, hey. This is Josh. Call me soon, dammit. I need to get an update for the old man before he cans me. I'm serious Mace. C'mon, man, call me soon."

Joshua ended the call and started his car. He backed out of his personal parking space. Then looking out of his window, he saw an opening, stepped on the gas, and entered the flow of traffic. "I wonder what Mace is up to in Chicago," he mused.

Little did Joshua know that Mace was exiting the shower and trying to answer his phone as Joshua was calling, but Mace was a bit too late and it rolled over to voice mail. Mace decided to get dressed while he waited for his IPhone to alert him that the caller had indeed left a voice mail. He wondered, "Now where are Linda and those tapes?" Then he recalled she had put them in the media room last night. Mace exited the man room and made a beeline for the projector.

Coming up the stairs, Linda greeted him and followed him to the couch. "Hello, sleepy head. I tried to awaken you several times, but I guess you must've had too much wine last night," she said smiling coyly. He

nodded affirmative, gave her a quick kiss, and plopped

down to begin. Linda joined him on the couch with hot

coffee and pushed the remote bringing the plasma screen

to life. A fuzzy image appeared similar to the ones on the

other tapes before finally coming into focus. "I'll watch

the people on the left side and you watch the right. Ok,

Linda?" Mace said. The tape ended and he was no closer

to finding Donald Roy Perkins than he was before arriving

in Milwaukee. Linda placed the last tape in the machine.

Mace was beginning to get that gnawing feeling in the pit

of his stomach, when he caught something out of the

corner of his eye on the screen. "Wait. Play that part

again," he told Linda.

"Did you see something, Mace?"

"I'm not sure, but I may have. Pause it right

there. Did you see that?" he asked. The frozen image was

two hands holding a note that read, "You're getting closer, Mace."

Running from a bounty hunter for ten months is very tiring. Having to change your appearance and locations only adds to the difficulty. For the first four months or so of his running, it was important for Donald Roy Perkins to discover as much as he could about who was on his tail. Often he could sense the closeness, and other times he knew he was safely out of range of his pursuer. Good thing he had someone on the inside feeding him information though he had no idea who this helper was. First he discovered that the best bounty hunter had been hired to bring him back to Las Vegas. Next, he was told that Mace was an expert at solving puzzles. It was after receiving this second piece of information that Donald Roy Perkins began to hatch a plan to use Mace Dugan to help prove his innocence. For reasons yet unknown, someone had gone through a lot of trouble to frame him. Unfortunately, the frame was made to fit him perfectly. His only option was to run while trying to solve the mystery and clear his name. Donald Roy decided to leave clues behind that alerted Mace as to where he was going. Also, he would tease Mace's deductive reasoning, using him to help solve the case. It had been working to perfection with the following him part, but not finding the real culprit. A new direction needed to be taken, and so in a brazen move, Donald Roy Perkins had stopped in front of one of the cameras in the Safe House bar with a note that read "You're getting closer, Mace." Now the trick was to find some way to enlist Mace's help without getting snared.

Perhaps a return to the Safe House tonight and another note stating his innocence would be just what the doctor ordered. So it had come down to two options: risk capture tonight to pass the note or flee and remain on the run. The second choice allowed him to continue evading the noose that seemed to be ever tightening around his neck, but the first had the better chance for long-term results. Donald Roy slipped into his most inconspicuous clothing; he checked the weather report and prepared his exit strategy from the Safe House. The predicted blizzard made the decision even easier. If things went wrong and his plan to enlist Mace's help failed, Donald Roy Perkins would escape using the storm to cover his tracks.

As Mace was getting dressed, he remembered the missed call. Enraged and baffled by the sudden realization that Donald Roy Perkins not only knew who he was, but how he thought, made him realize that he would now have to change his plans. This was not going to be an easy capture. He wasn't just chasing some ordinary everyday skipper. This guy was taunting him; seeing that note with his name on it sent a shiver down Mace's spine. It seemed as though the blood had stopped flowing in his veins.

Mace left the media room, headed to the man room, and grabbed his phone. Angrily he punched in the digits for Joshua Barton. He needed some answers, and he needed them yesterday. The only possible way that Donald Roy Perkins could know all of this was if someone were helping him. If he had to fly back to Vegas and strangle every lawyer in that firm, he was going to get some answers. Nobody plays "Mace the Ace" Dugan for a fool and gets away with it.

Before Joshua answered, Mace hung up the phone. This was no time to go off half-cocked; he needed to calm himself instead. He decided to soak in the hot tub next to the indoor pool and collect his thoughts. Linda agreed this was probably a wise decision. She quickly changed into her tiger striped bikini while Mace changed

into some borrowed trunks, and they went downstairs. It

was around 2 o'clock in the afternoon and the sun was

shining, so Linda opted to leave the sky light panels

opened to enjoy the view before darkness fell. She asked

if he wanted a margarita to which he normally would've

said yes, but this time he suggested, "How about some

hot tea instead?"

"Sure thing. That sounds like a great idea," Linda

agreed. "I'll just put some water on the stove to boil and

we can climb into the Jacuzzi while it heats."

The water temperature was so warm that Mace

melted into a peaceful relaxed state almost instantly. He

closed his eyes and he began retracing each step he'd

taken since receiving the call from Joshua asking for his

help. He was drifting into a state of semi consciousness

where things had just begun making sense when he was snapped back to the present by a whistling teapot.

His decision was already made though; he would return to the Safe House this evening and interview the bartenders, waitresses, and bouncers. "At long last," he thought, "I'll finally be ahead of Donald Roy Perkins." Maybe, just maybe he'd made a mistake and left something, anything behind that could help Mace catch him. A smile came to his face as he prepared to take a sip of Earl Grey tea. Oh, tonight was going to be good. He could feel the tide beginning to turn his way.

Chapter Two

Needle in a Haystack

Mace and Linda arrived at the Safe House just a few minutes before 7:00 p.m. She parked the car in the employees' covered garage. Snow was already falling heavily and the forecast predicted a white out before the night was over. The employee entrance was around the corner, hidden from view, and as Mace followed Linda inside, they paused for a moment allowing their eyes to adjust to the dim lighting in the hallway. Straight ahead was a flight of stairs with a door leading to a passageway. Along the corridor, which passed above the bar, were doors leading to the offices. Linda's office was the third door on the right where they entered and hung their jackets. Together they walked over to the video monitors. Linda grabbed Mace's hand before they settled into the overstuffed grey leather chairs and began sifting through the timesheets for last night's shift. Jamie Knight was the bartender; Darla Lyons, Karen Hirsch, Faith Abbey and Lyndsey Munroe were the waitresses, and Anthony Hall was the bouncer. James, big Jimbo Ourso and Chris Davis did the table busing, and Mark Wallace was the night manager. Mace decided to first interview the wait staff one girl at a time. Linda was confident that if they staggered the interviews and kept them short, none of the arriving customers would have to wait any longer than usual for service. Mace readily agreed, and Linda went downstairs to bring back the first worker for questioning.

Lyndsey came through the door and asked if he was the guy Linda said had some questions regarding last night. "Yes, I am, Lyndsey. I'm Mace. Please sit down and don't be nervous," Mace replied. "There was someone here last night, and I'm trying to find out if you served him."

"Oh, Mr. Mace, there was a big crowd in here last night, and I don't pay very close attention to the men," she said. "They tend to think I'm interested, and I have to fend them off all night, but I'll try."

"Great, Lyndsey," he replied. "That's all I'm asking you to do. Take a look at this picture and see if it sparks any memories."

Lyndsey studied it for a few seconds, and then shook her head and said, "Nope. Sorry. I don't remember seeing him last night." After Mace thanked her, he asked Lyndsey to tell Linda to send in the next person. As Lyndsey walked away, he saw exactly why she had to fend off advances all night, and it had nothing to do with whether or not she paid any attention to the bar patrons. Her costume of black, platform high heels, fishnet stockings, a bustier and fake fedora left little to the imagination. She looked like a moll who had been plucked from the mobsters of yesteryear.

Next to arrive at the door with a faint little knock was Karen, who apparently wasn't feeling well. She had a beet, red nose that she was lightly dabbing with a tissue in between raspy coughs which led Mace to ask how long she had been ill. "Oh," she said, "I've been fighting this for a couple of days. This happens to me every year around this time, but I'll be ok. I saw the doctor and got a shot and some medication yesterday before I came to work.

Linda said you wanted to talk to me." Mace showed her the picture of Donald Roy Perkins and asked her if she remembered seeing him last night. Linda held the photo and then she shook her head saying she didn't recall serving him last night. "Do you know what time it might have been?" she asked. "Probably around 9:30," Mace said.

"No, I'm sorry. Maybe it was Faith; she was covering my area around that time for me to go take medicine on my break."

"I see," Mace said. "Okay, thanks, Karen." Watching her leave in the same skimpy little outfit Lyndsey wore, he began to better understand why repeat customers poured into this place.

The next waitress to knock on the door next was Darla, a lovely little blonde with a very bubbly personality and the figure of a high school cheerleader. Mace assumed she had probably been very popular in school and asked her about it to ease into the interview. "Yes, I was a cheerleader in high school and college," she beamed as she spoke. "With this job, I get to dress really cute, and I can make over two hundred dollars a night in tips. That helps pay back my student loans, you know?

"Yes," he told her, "I understand completely."

"Plus, there are lots of hot guys that come in here," she added.

Mace raised the picture for her to look over and this caused her expression to become a serious scowl. Once she finished scanning the photo she looked back at him with her crystal blue eyes. Then she opened her mouth, smiled, and said, "Nope, I didn't see this guy last night. Maybe you should question me about if I'll be seeing you in the morning and how I like my eggs," she flirted. "What do you say? You're a great looking guy, and we could hook up when my shift is over if you're interested." Her finger lingered on her lips and she lightly sucked the tip as she locked eyes with his gaze.

Mace's eyes almost popped out of his head when he realized she was trying to pick him up. "Well," he stammered, "as interesting a proposition as that is, I've got more work to do; so, you're excused and may return to the bar." She leaned over the table exposing her cleavage. She placed hand on each breast and adjusted her top nearly popping out of her pink lace bra. Abruptly, she stood, turned around, and slapped her butt, "I'll be leaving tonight at midnight if you change your mind, stud. Let me know if you get your work finished. Then you can start working on me."

"Thank you, Darla; I believe I have everything I need right now," Mace replied. That invitation had left Mace nearly speechless and somewhat uncomfortable though flattered. Darla sure had the walk and the body made for that kind of suggestion to work. Mace walked to the bathroom to splash some cold water on his face before Faith arrived and saw him flushed and possibly out of sorts.

After drying his face and composing himself, Mace returned to the makeshift interrogation room where he found Faith already seated. Mace was a little surprised at her pink hair and heavy makeup, but on her it actually looked attractive.

"Hello Faith. I'm Mace. I've got a few questions for you," he stated.

Before Mace could finish the sentence, Darla poked her head back in and asked to see the picture again. Mace handed the photo to Darla once again and she reviewed it intently. "Yeah, that could be the guy who came in and asked where the secret exit was located.

After I showed him, he ordered a drink and stiffed me," she remarked. "But he didn't have blonde hair; it was brown, and he had a full beard. Those eyes though...that definitely could be him."

"Would you mind showing me the secret exit that you showed him?" Mace asked.

"No problem," she said. "I'll take you through it personally."

"Um, ok, just one minute, Darla. Thanks for coming in, Faith. If I have any more questions, I'll call you back. Okay?" Faith rose to leave the room and said, "Whatever works for you, man, will work for me, too."

Darla led the way as she and Mace headed for the secret exit. Mace was enjoying the view of Darla's backside instead of watching his own feet, and he almost tripped. Darla realized what had happened and she tossed a seductive glance over her shoulder. "Now don't go falling and hurting yourself, stud she teased. I'm taking you home with me tonight, and I don't want you incapacitated. Well not before we get to my place any way. You're going to need all of your energy for what I've got planned for us. It's right over here. See, just behind this old crate next to the wall."

As she bent over, Mace caught a glimpse of her garters and whistled. She entered first, and pulled him through, planting a deep, lingering kiss firmly on his lips while giving his butt a playful squeeze. "I just love your arms," she whispered into his ear. "What say you tease me a bit right now before I go back to waiting tables? The camera only points to the floor, so the girls can have secret sessions with their boyfriends, but I want you, and I want you now." She was very persistent, and although he found her extremely attractive, he pulled away saying, "I can't right now; I've got a job to do."

The entire event had a surreal quality, and Mace could feel his resistance weakening. The possibility of getting caught by someone snapped him back to his senses. Darla quickly kissed him again causing him to almost lose his balance. She rose to her feet and said, "That was the quick one, but later on we can take all the time we want. Now, I'll see you for the encore at midnight, right?" All he could muster was, "Yeahhh."

Had this really just happened? Did a beautiful cheerleader, half his age, try to seduce him in the dark corridor of a spy bar? "Man, my life is good," he thought while gathering his composure before exiting the secret room and returning to the club floor. That's when he remembered her saying the camera only pointed to the floor. Mace turned around and went back to see it for himself. He found it exactly as she had described. The camera seemed to have been adjusted downward intentionally. He scribbled a quick note saying, "I'm going to get you, Mace Dugan," held it near the camera as he suspected Donald Roy Perkins had, and then headed to the video surveillance room for a look.

When he arrived, the monitor still showed the room as dark and unoccupied. Replaying the tape, he saw the note; it looked eerily similar to the one Donald Roy Perkins had held the night before. That was definitely the spot, and thankfully there was no video or audio evidence of his encounter with Darla. The only sound on the tape was spy music piped in to enhance the ambiance of the bar.

Linda noticed the display on the monitor as she entered the office. "Oh no, Mace, look at that note. He's here!" Mace chuckled and told her that he had written that as a test to prove this was the camera angle from the tape they had watched that afternoon at her house.

"Well, I feel foolish," Linda said.

"Don't, Linda. You had no way of knowing I had done that," Mace replied. Okay. Let's change the subject she said, "Jamie, the bartender last night, is waiting for you in the spare office."

"Okay. Thanks," he said, "I'll be right in to see her." Linda was very good at finding and hiring beautiful women to work at the Safe House. It's a wonder that the place ever had an off night cash wise. Jamie was probably 5 feet 5 inches tall with sparkling green eyes and typical Slavic features. Her words were spoken with a heavy accent.

"Hallo, I am Yamie" is what he heard. "Hello, Jamie, would you like to sit?" he asked. Mace showed her the picture and she replied, "Maybe so. Der was a guy in here last night who looked something like dis, but he had full beard and darker hair."

"Did you see where he went or what he did?" he asked.

"Vell, I tink he had a beer, talked to Mark the manager, then paid his bill and left." Jamie stated.

"Wonderful, Jamie. Thanks so much. You've been a great help." Mace told her.

"You're velcome," she said. "I can go now?"

"Yes, you may go," was the reply. "Goodbye Jamie.

"Goodbye Mr. Mace".

Little did Mace know that Linda had been dead on the money when she thought that Donald Roy Perkins was actually there. Mace had been so preoccupied with Darla, the camera, and interviews that he had completely overlooked Donald Roy Perkins sitting at the bar watching him. He had no idea that Perkins had arrived at the Safe House before Linda and himself, and was doing some recon work of his own. He had watched Mace go into the secret exit with Darla and then saw him hurry up the stairs. It was at this time Donald Roy decided to make his move.

Mark had just arrived and was making the rounds in the bar, checking supplies and staffing when he was called over by Donald Roy Perkins for a quick conversation.

"Hey, I remember you from last night, sir. How are you this evening? Is everything alright?" Mark inquired. "You know," Donald Roy said as he rocked his hand back and forth, "So, so. Would you do me a favor please, Mark?" Donald Roy asked.

"What's that?" Mark asked.

"I've got a special note here for the owner, and I was wondering if you'd mind delivering it to her when you see her?" Donald Roy asked.

"Not a problem, sir. I'd be delighted to," Mark said. Donald Roy Perkins handed the note to Mark and then slipped right out the secret exit he had used to escape a scant 24 hours ago. Donald Roy knew that it wouldn't take very long before the note was delivered to Linda and his plan would begin to put into action.

Mark saw Linda five minutes or so after receiving the note and handed it to her retelling the conversation he'd had with the patron. He piqued her interest after saying the guy had been in the night before and just had to stop back by before leaving town. Linda opened the note and almost fainted.

Mark asked her if she was okay, and she said, "Get me to my office immediately, please." Mark came bolting into the spare office, "Something's wrong with Linda! She told me to come get you."

"Where is she?" Mace inquired with a worried voice.

"In her office," Mark answered. Hurriedly Mace opened the door and found Linda white as a ghost. "What's wrong?" he asked.

Unable to even speak; she pointed to the note on her desk. Mace retrieved the note and then unfolded it. There in bold print he read these words, "I'm not guilty. Someone is trying to frame me for the deaths of my wife and daughter. I loved them both. Please help me find out who is behind this and bring them to justice for me and my family, Mace." The final stanza of the note stated that he was on his way back to where this whole thing started, Las Vegas. He was also imploring Mace to follow and team up with him. It was signed Donald Roy Perkins, an innocent man.

Mace's body went numb. The paper slipped from his fingers as he crumpled into the chair. Could this be true? If this were true, who was responsible for the deaths of Donald Roy's family? Why was this heinous act being played out with him as an unwitting participant? These and so many other questions flooded his mind. What was he going to do now? Should he even believe Donald Roy Perkins' note? Could this, somehow, be a trick or, worse yet, a trap? That crystal clear vision he'd had earlier in Linda's hot tub was miles away now. Why was Donald Roy returning to Las Vegas? Surely he knew whoever was responsible for this had to figure he would return sometime, right?

This was quite a dilemma. Mace felt like he was trying to solve a Rubik's cube with no matching colors. He got a cold wrenching feeling in his stomach as if he'd eaten bad food and about to be sick from it. "Calm down, Mace," he instructed himself. "Breathe in. Breathe out. Just try to relax." It was time to start thinking more like a detective and less like a skip tracer trying to apprehend a bail jumper.

Mace's first stop would be the public library to review the case history. This, of course, meant he was returning to Las Vegas, home sweet home, where he could research the case from old newspaper files. Mace decided to call the airlines immediately to check on a flight. He grabbed the phone and dialed the toll free number for the airline. The soft female voice on the other end of the line told him Northwest Airlines had a flight at 7:00 p.m. tomorrow night, "Would you like me to book a seat for you, sir?"

"Yes," he said. "The name is Mace Dugan."

"I see, Mr. Dugan. Will that be first class or coach?"

"First class, please," he said. "Here is my World Perks frequent flyer number"

"Okay. Let me make sure I have this right. That's one first class seat on tomorrow's 7:00 p.m. Northwest Airlines flight from Milwaukee to Las Vegas, Nevada. Is that correct"?

"Yes," he said, "that's correct."

"Very well, then, Mr. Dugan. You'll need to arrive 90 minutes before your scheduled departure to guarantee this spot and clear security. Will that be a

problem?"

"Nope. No problem at all."

"Okay, then. Can I help you with anything else?"

"No, that's all. Thank you," he said.

"Thank you for calling Northwest Airlines. Have a

pleasant evening Mr. Dugan. Goodbye." Okay, now that

the flight had been booked, what should he do to enjoy

his last night in Milwaukee?

Mace decided to continue interviewing the

remaining staff to further establish last night's events and

Donald Roy's m.o. The initials m.o. are Latin for modus

operandi or the more easier understood, patterns.

When Linda discovered he was staying one more

night, she tried to rearrange her schedule but was

unsuccessful. She said if he wanted she would call Albert, the security guard, and clear him through so he could stay in the man room. She, however, had to drive to Chicago to meet her stranded friend Janice. Mace told Linda not to worry about him, that he would probably get a hotel room before leaving for the airport tomorrow. Linda kissed Mace goodbye, and they embraced. Neither one wanted to let go. Linda gazed into Mace's eyes and her expression warmed him to his heart. Mace returned the stare but knew she had to leave for Chicago and he had more interviews. One last kiss and Linda headed for her car.

Mace told her to be careful driving in the winter storm and Linda assured him that she would. She also told him that she enjoyed their time together and suggested maybe they could get together again sometime soon if he felt the same way about her. Mace nodded in agreement and said he'd give her a call when this was over.

Little did Linda know, nor would he divulge, but Mace had already developed seriously strong feelings for this beautiful woman. He couldn't dare mouth the words, but felt he could be falling for her. As she walked to her car, he realized that it was getting close to 10:00 p.m. In two hours the bar would be closing.

On his way back upstairs, he stopped to show Faith the photograph of Donald Roy Perkins. "I don't recognize him," she said. When Mace mentioned that he might have a beard and darker hair, she perked up, but then said she didn't think that was him.

Anthony Delgado, the bouncer, was a thirty-something man of Italian descent. He told Mace that last night was peaceful and quiet. "When it gets this cold," he said, "most people don't have the desire or energy to start fights, and we rarely have any trouble here, anyway. This is one of the easiest jobs I've ever held and Ms. Linda is a great boss."

James and Chris were of no help either. Their focus was the dirty dishes and whatever change the waitresses left for them as an incentive to keep their tables bussed and ready for new customers.

The last interview was with Mark, the night manager. Donald Roy had apparently sat at the bar near the stool Mark was occupying and engaged him in conversation concerning the secret passageways of the bar. Mark mentioned that there were hidden entrances, exits, and dead end rooms to confuse any would be assailants following a spy. The idea for this place was that the American spies knew where all of the hidden places were, so that they could out maneuver foreign spies and turn the tables on them. The concept of the bar was actually the brainchild of a man believed to have been an ex-CIA operative, or so the story was told. Mark and Donald Roy spoke most of the night until Mark had to leave to check the kitchen for closing. When Mark returned, Donald Roy was gone.

As the clock began to chime the first of 12 bells, Mace saw Darla counting her tips and closing out her customers' credit cards. She saw him watching her, looked straight at him, and licked her lips slowly as if she were a cannibal and he was her next meal. As a man, he would have to say he was more than a little intrigued, so he returned the gesture. She smiled and pointed to the secret compartment where they had just been a few hours ago. Mace got the message loud and clear. If he didn't keep his word and their date, Darla would let Linda know what had happened in there between the two of them.

Actually, he thought if he let her come to his hotel, or if they wound up at her place, he'd feign a headache and perhaps keep her at bay. Darla came by and told him to meet her outside at the workers' entrance in 15 minutes and that he'd better be ready to give her the time of her life or be prepared to spend his last breath trying.

While he waited, Mace saw Darla exiting the employees' entrance. She was wearing a long, brown leather coat, she flashed him, exposing her micro mini skirt, black fishnet stockings and plunging top. A golden heart on a chain hung from her pierced navel and she gave the wickedest smile he had ever seen on a woman of her age. Mace had a feeling that even though she was 20 years his junior, she could teach him some new tricks if his heart and body could hold out.

She told him to follow her Jaguar to the apartment and to get ready for the single most incredible night of his life. When she pulled out of the parking garage, he tucked in behind her in his rental. The moon lit up the streets like the neon lights of Vegas, and he found his mind drifting back to his hometown.

The falling snow had blanketed the town softening all the city's harsh edges. Christmas carols played through the speakers on the street. Winter displays decorated the store windows, and holiday lights blinked messages of good will to all.

Darla seemed intent on testing Mace's desire to stay behind her as she went through one caution light after another; gunning the engine and causing the exhaust to smoke. Just as he was prepared to give up the

pursuit, she put on her right blinker and turned into an

apartment complex. Weaving around the turns and

parked cars, she found an open spot just in front of the F

building. Mace found one not far away and eased into it.

He switched off his headlights and ignition, climbed out of

his car and pressed the alarm set on the car fob. The

parking lights blinked twice rapidly and the horn chirped

indicating the car was protected.

Darla pointed to the door marked F2 and waited

for Mace on the stoop. When he arrived, she grabbed his

hand and snuggled him tightly before pushing open the

door and pulling him inside. Mace had the thought that

he might be a entering the web of a black widow spider

and he was the main course.

Inside Darla's apartment Mace was pleasantly

surprised to discover an understated, yet elegant living

room. A cocoa brown leather sectional, wooden rocking

chair, cherry wood coffee table, two lamp stands and a

television were cozily arranged. The copies of

Mademoiselle and *Cosmopolitan* magazines on the coffee

table alluded to her sense and style. Scanning the room,

he noticed incense and scented candles throughout the

living area. Pillows, throw rugs and pictures of Darla with

people of varying ages and in different locations were

placed around. She shed her coat and took his as well

hanging them in her front closet. When she returned she

asked Mace what he'd like to drink. He inquired as to

what she was having and she seductively purred, "I'm

having you. Aren't I?"

Mace decided to have Irish eggnog as did Darla. In

the kitchen he helped her get the mugs and whiskey as

she retrieved the carton of eggnog from the fridge. After

she filled the mugs and placed them in the microwave, Darla asked Mace how he'd come to be a bounty hunter.

Mace told her that he had blended the two activities he loved most, puzzles and travel, and had married them into his career. Darla was slightly reluctant to tell Mace how she had become a waitress when he asked her. It wasn't so much that she had wanted to be a waitress she explained, but while she was in college a friend suggested it to her, and her first night reaped over $200 in tips. After graduation, she sent out resumes but hadn't found anything as lucrative as waitressing at the Safe House Bar, so she'd kept working there.

The timer on the microwave beeped and Darla removed the eggnog, added the whiskey and whipped cream and then asked Mace if he liked her outfit or if she should change in something else.

Mace suggested that what she had on was more than

doing the trick for him as long as she was comfortable.

Darla handed Mace one of the mugs then made a toast

to having one helluva night together before clinking their

two mugs together. The leftover whipped cream from the

sip made a moustache on Darla's lips and they both

laughed. Mace slipped over and licked the tasty treat

from her lips. They kissed and then settled next to each

other on the sofa.

Mace and Darla spent the early morning talking

and drinking. The pictures of her family made him

wonder what it was like to have siblings. Vacation photos

with her parents, kid sister and baby brother in Hawaii,

Disneyland and the Grand Canyon caused her eyes get a

little misty. This beautiful, young woman had a nurturing

side that he hadn't guessed existed. She told him about

the tattoo over her heart, a bleeding, broken heart with

blood droplets down to her rib. This was her way of keeping her little brother, Ronnie, close and always on her mind. Ronnie had died from cancer when he was only five years old. Mace held her and comforted her until they both fell fast asleep. Darla slept with her head on Mace's shoulder until 12:20 in the afternoon.

The sound of the neighbor's music awakened them. "What we need is a shower and something to eat," she said. "Mace I'm sorry I passed out on you after promising to give the night of our lives Darla bemoaned.

"Yes, I'm starving, too, Darla, but I've got to be at the airport by 5 to return the rental car, so there isn't much time," Mace explained. "It's okay sweetheart. We were both pretty tired and those Irish coffees did the rest. Do you know of a good restaurant on the way where we can grab a quick bite?"

The two exchanged phone numbers after they both showered and dressed. Each one promised the other that they would stay in touch.

Despite his initial reservations of going out with Darla, she had turned out to be quite a wonderful woman. She suggested her favorite Thai restaurant. Mace followed her there; they walked right in and got the best table in the house. The host called her by name and remarked how she seemed to be glowing today. She thanked him for the compliment and they sat to peruse the menu. Once seated, Darla told Mace that she ate there at least twice weekly because Thai food is loaded with nutrients and is low in calories. She recommended the volcano chicken, and he happily agreed. They enjoyed the delicious meal and talked of the events that had brought them to this point and place in time. Eventually she needed to get ready for work and he had to return the rental car to the airport.

After a nice kiss and a long hug goodbye she left for her apartment and Mace headed for I-794. What appeared to be plenty of time to catch his flight soon evaporated into no time to spare. The line to return the rented BMW was longer than expected due to a shortage of tellers at the front desk. Linda phoned and asked if she could see Mace off at the terminal, and he said of course she could; that would be very nice of her.

As Mace ran through the airport, he realized he might miss his flight. A multitude of scenarios were playing out in his head like songs on a playlist; as soon as one ended another would begin. It was a never-ending circle that wouldn't allow his mind to rest. Though he had no idea who was in charge of this show, they had him dancing like a puppet on a string. Someone was orchestrating this and had succeeded in keeping him unaware of the real purpose of chasing Donald Roy Perkins.

Mace arrived at the gate as the last boarding call went out, he checked in. Linda called out to him, "Mace, over here!" They briefly embraced, kissed, and she told him to call her when he arrived at his destination and was in for the night and he nodded he would. The gate attendant said, "Sir, if you want to make this flight, you have to board immediately." Mace turned from Linda, refusing to look back and passed through the door leading out to a waiting 747. Once inside, he found his seat, stowed the gym bag he'd carried in the overhead compartment and settled in for the long flight home. The captain announced they were next in line for takeoff. As his eyes begin to close, the jet begin rumbling forward down the runway headed into the dark night sky.

The sound of the landing gear being lowered awakened Mace from his slumber. He raised the window blind and looked out the window. Just off in the distance, he could see the glow from the lights of the famous Las Vegas strip. Even though it was almost 11:00 p.m., the storied Vegas nightlife was in full swing, and somewhere amongst all of those people were Joshua Barton, Tonya his office secretary, a possible unknown assassin or two, Donald Roy Perkins, and hopefully the answers to this mystery.

The flight attendant came by, smiled, and said, "You'll have to raise your seat to its full and upright position before we land sir." Before Mace could even reach for the button to comply, she leaned over, pressed against him, and whispered into his ear, "I'll be here for a three day furlough. I noticed you aren't wearing a wedding ring on your finger. Maybe we could get together before I have to fly out again" she suggested. Without waiting for his answer, she slipped him a piece of paper. "Here's my number, Mace. I checked your name on the flight manifest. I hope you don't mind," she said as she winked her deep blue eyes at him. "Call me. Okay? I'm certain we could have a great time together."

He took the paper and stuffed it into his shirt pocket. "I'm sure we could, too, Amber" he replied. Shortly after this encounter with Amber the wheels made that familiar screeching sound when they touched the runway. Mace was jostled in his seat as the plane began to slow from its flight speed to taxi speed. It was a fairly smooth ride to the terminal center. After the plane came to rest, the lights came on and the pilot came over the intercom welcoming the passengers to Las Vegas and giving the local time and temperature. Calmly the passengers in coach waited as the first class section emptied from the plane. Amber waved, smiled, and wished everyone a nice stay in Las Vegas, as she coyly commented, "Remember. What happens in Vegas stays in Vegas."

Boy, if he had a nickel for every time Mace had heard that phrase, he just might be as wealthy as Linda. Mace laughed heartily, exited the jet way, and headed up the terminal where his eyes tried to adjust to the bright lights. The smell of fresh coffee and airport food filled his nostrils as he neared the escalator. The aisle was partially crowded though it was nearing midnight. Planes constantly bring in anxious gamblers and visitors all night long; and tonight was no exception.

The nap Mace had taken during the four-hour flight had left him feeling alert and refreshed. As he drew near the baggage turnstile, he spied Tonya. She didn't look particularly pleased to see him though. Mace guessed it was due to the late hour of his arrival and the realization that with his return, her 10- month semi-vacation would be coming to an end. The tone of his voice as he briefed her told her immediately that they would be very busy. It would take some digging to find the truth from this stack of misinformation. Mace wasn't sold on Donald Roy's claim of innocence yet, but it did have some points that required investigation.

Mace's secretary Tonya had received the hastily composed text message detailing his flight information. She was there waiting to pick him up at baggage claim and drive him to his condo near the outskirts of town. It was nothing approaching Linda's lifestyle, but it suited his needs just fine.

Mace could still see that look on Linda's face before he passed through the boarding gate at breakneck speed. Her eyes were pleading with him to stay and help her run the Safe House. Though he suspected she was

everything and more he could ask for in a woman, he

knew the real Mace too well. Shortly after agreeing to

stay with her, he'd get that old familiar calling to head out

on the trail of some skipper and solve mysteries. Yes, it

was better that he left her behind in Milwaukee and

stayed true to himself and his curious nature. He knew

that he was not a one-woman kind of man. No, his

motto, instead, had been that there were many different

types of women in the world and he wasn't sure that he

had tasted enough of them to settle on just one yet.

Tonya informed him that she had already

retrieved his bags and that her car was waiting outside.

They hurried because she had parked in a loading zone

where there was a 30-minute time limit, and airport

police lived to catch people exceeding it. Tonya assured

Mace that she wasn't paying the $250 fine if he caused her to be ticketed.

Automatic doors opened as they approached and the stale, muggy night air seemed harder to breathe than Mace remembered. "The body has an incredible ability to adapt to its surroundings," he thought. He dropped into the passenger seat of Tonya's Ford Mustang convertible and playfully pointed out the window saying, "Home, Jane." She scowled at him and it reminded him how much she hated being called anything except her given name. Tonya wasn't one of those girls that liked being called by pet names and she'd told Mace numerous times. Without another word, she pulled away from the curb. Mace realized instantly just how much he missed that BMW and how much hotter the winters were in Vegas compared to Milwaukee or Chicago. No snow or cold winds here, just a nice warm temperature and soft breezes blowing though the palms. Good to be home.

Tonya dropped Mace at home, and he waved goodbye. "Remember to pick me up in the morning," he said as he removed his suitcases from her trunk. Tonya waved when the trunk closed and she was off into the night.

After Mace piled the clothes from his suitcase near the washer, he lowered the thermostat and fell into bed. He grudgingly set the alarm on the clock radio to awaken him in about 9 hours. Since he always slept in the nude, Mace forced himself to get up and peel off his clothes and shoes. The light on the nightstand was blinding and he needed to use the bathroom anyway, so he rose stubbing his toe on the doorjamb half way there. Before returning to bed, he set the house alarm then turned off the lamp on his nightstand. Just as his head began to sink into the pillow, the memory of his

unbelievable experiences in Milwaukee with Linda filled

his mind and he drifted off to sleep smiling. He was still

dreaming when the radio blared in his ears. The red LED's

showed 9:00 a.m., and he knew he needed to get up and

get dressed so Tonya wouldn't have to wait. Mace

showered and made breakfast. As he languished over his

second cup of coffee, he heard the horn outside and

opened the door to see Tonya as expected. After setting

the alarm, he grabbed his favorite pair of Maui Jim

sunglasses, closed the door, twisted the dead bolt, and

shoved the keys into the front pocket of his jeans.

The drive to the library was short, but the traffic

was heavy with people on their way to their destinations.

Horns honked and songs blared from the many

convertibles around them. In other words, this was just a

typical day in Las Vegas. They arrived at the Las Vegas

Public Library around 11 a.m. and found an empty parking

spot. They exited the car and made their way to the front

door. Although there were almost always vagrants

hanging around outside and the air reeked of body odor

and garbage, the reference section was still one of the

best around. They strolled up to the librarian and asked

where they could find the newspapers from 11 months

ago. She told them that anything that old would be

found only on microfilm. They set out for the viewing

room and she followed behind them to explain the proper

usage of the microfilm viewer.

The librarian showed them the process to load

the film and use the buttons to advance and rewind

tapes. Each nodded understanding and she left them

alone to begin their research. Five hours later they

discovered something very peculiar regarding these

machines. Staring causes eye strain when trying to stop

at the correct page of the newspaper. They decided to take a break to allow their eyes to rest for a short while. After some Mexican food and discussion, they returned to the little viewing room finally getting their first piece of encouraging information from the microfilm. According to the newspaper, the prosecutor had a flimsy circumstantial case at best against Donald Roy Perkins. It seemed the police hadn't found any hard evidence implicating anyone positively. So it had fallen back to the old tried and true method of blame the spouse. Although Robin West, the journalist had been objective in his article, his boss had fired him anyway. The tenor of the article hadn't met with the approval of the editor. A journalist should always write the story the way the editor instructs, or be prepared to face the consequences, but Robin refused to give Donald Roy Perkins the label of murderer without concrete proof.

Mace decided he would begin by meeting with Robin West. Tonya made a quick call to ask if Mace could talk with Robin about his story, and he agreed to the meeting. They left the library after finding the last known address for Robin and headed out in search of the next piece of the puzzle.

Mace peered into the rear view mirror and caught a glimpse of what he thought was a tail car about 3 or so vehicles back. The first lesson in surveillance training was to not be obvious and wind up being spotted following a target. With Mace seeing this tail so quickly after leaving the library he was certain that this person was either being intentionally obvious or else it was an amateur. He alerted Tonya and she asked, "What do we do, Mace?"

Popular opinion holds that the one being pursued should increase speed and swerve through traffic attempting to lose or outrun the tail. This is not necessary in most cases; if the driver being pursued would simply make a turn where there is a large amount of foot traffic, and slow down, the passenger could exit the car unseen.

Tonya waited until Mace instructed and then she turned through a heavy foot traffic are. She slowed and Mace hopped from the passenger seat, exited the car and blended into the crowd. Mace made his way to the curb and watched to see a dark blue Ford sedan with a driver wearing a suit and tie following Tonya's Mustang. The pursuer was holding a video camera in his hand as he drove, thus confirming Mace's suspicion that he was indeed an amateur.

Mace called Tonya's cell phone, told her to run errands with her tail, and that he'd go see Robin West alone. Mace stepped to the curb, raised a hand and gave out a loud whistle. The cab stopped in front of him and he settled into the back seat. Mace closed the door, gave the driver Robin's address and they set out for the other side of town.

The mobile home lot on the edge of Las Vegas that Robin called home was a fairly nice place. Each lot was neatly trimmed and had a concrete area for the bar-b-que pit or picnic table. Several people were having a cookout as the cabbie pulled in and dropped Mace off. After he exited the cab Mace smelled that all too familiar aroma of lighter fluid and smoke. He could see a blue Nissan Frontier in the driveway and the lights were on in the kitchen at Robin's address. Mace climbed the 5 steps to the entrance and took several deep breaths. He steeled himself for the inevitable onslaught of venom he was certain would be hurled in his direction and knocked twice on the door. To his surprise, an average looking fellow with brown hair and a short scar on his left cheek opened the door and asked, "Who are you?"

"My name is Mace Dugan. My secretary called a little while ago mentioning that I'm interested in asking you some questions about the Donald Roy Perkins case."

"What's so interesting about a story I wrote almost a year ago? One that got me fired, I might add," Robin said, lifting his faded Arizona State baseball cap to scratch his head.

Mace explained to Robin that he had been hired to track Donald Roy Perkins after he jumped bail. Recent events had him verifying the validity of some left out information that could place his guilt in question. "I was hoping you could help me clear up a few details," Mace said.

Robin invited him in and asked if he'd like a beer. The door closed behind Mace to reveal a rather nice home. The TV had been muted, and the Lazy boy chair had a black and white puppy straining its eyes over the arm peering out at Mace. The dog was wagging its tail and it was making a thumping sound as it beat against the chair cover. The sofa appeared to be sagging just a bit in the middle and it too was covered. Mace assumed that the coverings were there for the dog more than anything else. A bookcase with journalism awards and framed articles were scattered about the living room. It was obvious to Mace that Robin had been a well-respected member of the press prior to the Donald Roy Perkins article.

Robin said that they could talk while he finished making burgers for the grill party. As he spoke, Robin returned to pressing out the circular shapes of fresh ground chuck for supper and Mace took a seat at the bar. Robin reached into the refrigerator handed Mace an ice cold Heineken and got one for himself, as well. They popped the caps off, and Mace took a long, deep swig of the ice-cold beer.

Robin said, "Mace, you're the second person to come calling at my house about this story lately. Mace asked if Robin remembered the name of the other person. No I don't but hang on a second Robin said. He wiped his hands, and began shuffling around in a drawer. Presently Robin handed Mace a business card with the name Michael Winters, private investigator printed on it. Mace asked what they had discussed. Robin told him flatly that he had said nothing. "I didn't trust him; my instincts told me this guy was a liar," Robin said. "I've interviewed hundreds of people in my career, and something about this guy didn't add up to me."

Slowly sipping the beer, Mace asked him question after question while never really getting to the one he wanted Robin to answer. Robin was a gracious host and he willingly answered each question Mace posed to him. Robin waited until he was almost ready to head out the door when he stopped, looked Mace directly in the eye and said, "When are you going to ask me the real question?" Mace answered him by asking, "Do you have any proof that Donald Roy Perkins is innocent?" There it was, out on the table, finally.

"That's the one I've been waiting for, Mace. While it may not be accepted as legal proof, I've got this audiotape that was anonymously sent to me that certainly brings his guilt into question. Let me get it for you so you can hear it for yourself." Robin opened a small wall safe behind a picture of his golden retriever, Lady, and handed Mace the telephone answering machine tape.

"What's on here, Robin?" Mace inquired.

"Take this and have it analyzed," Robin replied. "I don't want to prejudice your opinion of the worth of the recording beforehand. Nobody else seems interested, but promise me that you'll get it back to me when you're done. Okay?"

"Sure thing," Mace replied, "and thank you Robin."

"No problem Mace. As a journalist, I can't stand seeing someone get railroaded. Now, I've gotta get back to my friends and get these burgers cooked before they lynch me," he chuckled.

Mace pulled out his phone and called for a cab to return him to the office. Standing outside listening to burgers sizzling and music playing, Mace finished off his beer while he waited for the taxi. Robin had quite a crew over there. The dancing, singing, drinking and overall partying almost made Mace wish he could stay longer; but duty was calling. Once inside the cab Mace's thoughts began to turn to the five W questions every detective and journalist is taught to ask: who, what, where, when and why. He'd get to the how later he mused. He gave the address to his office to the cabbie, waved to Robin and his gang, and then sat back mulling the real possibility that Donald Roy Perkins just might be innocent after all.

Chapter Three

Back and Forth

Mace called Tonya to ask her location and to see if she was still being followed. She laughed and said that the guy gave up after her first three stops. Apparently he wasn't a fan of the dry cleaners, nail salons, and dress boutiques. He saw she had spotted him, so he jumped into his car and tore off down the road. She kept a close watch in the rear view mirror and made her way back to the office where she waited for her next instructions.

Mace told her to call Glen Stevens, his old Navy buddy and resident audio specialist, and alert him that he had a tape that needed his expertise ASAP. Tonya said she'd get right on that.

The cab driver turned onto the street where Mace's office was located and immediately Mace felt something in his gut telling him to get out early. He told the cabbie, "Pull over. I'll walk the remaining two blocks." He's learned early in like to trust the hackles on the back of his neck. Mace opened the cab door and began to slowly search the street for anything seemingly out of place. The driver took the fare and Mace slipped from the back door. His eyes continued scanning for clues.

Walking nonchalantly up the sidewalk, he first noticed a guy across from his office wearing night vision binoculars. Each puff of his cigarette illuminated his facial features in the dark. He appeared young, late twenties maybe, with a goatee and gold tooth. A short distance up and across the street was another guy pretending to be a wino. He gave himself away by having a visible wired earpiece and sitting directly under the street lamp.

Who were these guys and why were they watching him? Did Robin's tape really mean Donald Roy Perkins was innocent? It surely was looking that way. Mace grabbed his iPhone and told Glen to pick him up at their hangout instead of the office. When Glen pulled up outside of Guidry's Bar, Mace jumped into his car, and they went to his lab to hear the tape for the first time.

Mace noticed Glen was wearing glasses and his golden hair was beginning to thin. Glen looked at Mace and said, "If you say one word, Mace, just one word, I'll throw you out on the street." Mace laughed and said, "Who? Me? Say anything about what?"

"Listen, smart ass, my doctor told me that since I'm in my forties, I need these to keep from straining my eyes and ending the day with a headache," Glen replied.

"OK," Mace said,"but what happened to your hair?" Glen punched Mace's arm and said, "Damn, man! It's good to see you. What's new, buddy?" Mace began to tell him of his experiences with Linda, and Glen replied, "Same old Mace; always the ladies' man."

As they pulled into the parking lot at Glen's Mace was reminded of a case they had worked on several years ago. Glen had been able to isolate the sound of a single gunshot that had been masked in the background by a car backfiring. This solitary piece of evidence had kept Tim Waller, a good friend of theirs, out of the electric chair for murder.

Tim owned a gun store, and ever since that time, he'd given them huge discounts on any handguns they needed. Tim even looked the other way when they needed something more in the line of military weaponry.

Glen's love of music had led him to become a sonar technician in the Navy, and he also provided mixing services for several of the local casinos' sound stages now that he had retired. Glen's place looked nothing like a sophisticated audio lab from the outside, and that was just the way he liked it. The two Navy buddies exited the car making certain no one had followed them and slipped inside the front door without turning on any lights. Glen took the tape and made his way across the room where he turned on his desk lamp. He placed soft white cotton gloves on his hands and then loaded the tape into his digital analyzer. In a process commonly known as "cleaning up the audio," he isolated out all of the background noises one by one until the only thing left was the vocal speaking range. What they heard was two people talking about framing the pigeon for murdering his wife and daughter to keep his mouth shut. Then the message was garbled for a few seconds before a familiar

female voice spoke and said, "Now don't screw this up.

I've got a lot of money tied up in this, and I don't want

you guys making a mess of things." Mace was certain

he'd heard this voice before but couldn't put a name on

it. That was all there was except for static and what

sounded like a car horn. Glen played the tape back several

times at varying speeds to ensure he hadn't missed

anything. After gleaning everything possible from the

short 30 or so seconds of audio, he sat down, took off his

gloves and jotted a few notes on a tablet at his desk.

Well, there it was, maybe not legal proof but

enough to warrant a talk with Mr. Donald Roy Perkins to

find out why he was being framed to remain quiet. Glen

assured Mace that the tape was authentic and not some

cleverly crafted ruse made to throw them off track. Each

man trusted the other with his life, so they concluded that

there was definitely more to this case than met the eye. Additional research and investigation were certainly warranted.

Trying to figure out how to get in contact with Donald Roy Perkins without scaring him away was Mace's next dilemma. Perhaps if he told Joshua that he had some new information, word would trickle out through whatever leak had been feeding information to Donald Roy Perkins for the last 11 months. It's good to have friends to use as sounding boards. Glen and Mace decided that this idea was probably the best bet to get a sit down with Donald Roy Perkins. So at one o'clock in the afternoon, Mace picked up his cell phone and dialed Joshua's number. After he answered Mace said, "There is definitely some doubt as to the guilt of Donald Roy Perkins, and we needed to confer with the judge and prosecutor to discuss some new evidence that has just come to light."

Joshua wanted all of the details, but Mace told him he wasn't willing to discuss it over the phone and that a meeting needed to be scheduled for midnight to get the proof. Mace told Joshua he needed to start making those phone calls and to let him know when the meeting was arranged. Joshua reluctantly hung up the phone and Glen said, "The clock is ticking now." They had figured maybe 48 hours from the phone call until Joshua could arrange his meeting, so Mace expected to be hearing from Donald Roy Perkins before then. Since Joshua's job was still on the line, Mace knew he could count on his promptness regarding it.

Since Mace was holding the trump card, the audiotape, he decided to play his hunch like a poker game. When playing poker, it truly doesn't matter that much what cards are being held. What's important is what the other players in the game THINK is being held. Living in Vegas he'd learned many lessons about bluffing and watching for tells, little signs that gamblers repeat each time they have a certain hand or are bluffing. One player may touch her ear ring or push up her glasses every time she has two aces in her hand. Perhaps another may cough twice whenever he is bluffing. Good players learn to read these signs and use them against the weaker players. This time Mace was in a game with a man's future in his hands, and he didn't even know who all the players were.

Lacking this knowledge meant Mace was playing the game handicapped. The only tell he had discovered was that every time he had gotten a piece of information, Donald Roy Perkins soon had it too. Every place he'd followed him for the past 11 months, Donald Roy already knew when Mace was coming and where he was going. So Mace decided he was going use a tactic known as misinformation to flush the players from their hiding places. Sometimes an unexpected bluff can cause the players to rethink the way they are playing the game. For Mace, the game was finding the truth by raising the stakes, going all in, and thereby forcing the others to make a decision. Would they stay with their cards and test his hand to see if he is bluffing, or would they fold and let Mace take the whole pot?

If he was right and this worked, he'd have the upper hand and could then cause this house of cards to be exposed for a sham. If, however, they had expected this play, he could be walking into a very big trap. Mace's experience had trained him to believe the best and always plan for the worst.

They left Glen's lab and headed over to see Tim at his store, Accuracy Gun Shop, Inc. Las Vegas was starting to get into full night mode with limousines carrying high rollers up and down the strip. Call girls were working both sides of the street. Even though prostitution was illegal in Las Vegas, undercover policewomen dressed as hookers still arrested their fair share of visitors for solicitation anyway. One such officer was standing on the street corner wearing a camel half fur jacket, heavy makeup, skin-tight spandex pants, platform shoes, and a fake red wig. She was bending through the passenger window, chewing gum, and flicking her extra long fingernails against the doorframe of the car parked next to Mace and Glen at the stoplight. Mace alerted the poor, clueless guy that she was a setup and he was about to become the victim of a sting. He thanked Mace and rolled up his window while the hooker flipped him off cursing a blue streak. She continued yelling something about Mace being lucky the light had changed or he'd be arrested for...the sound trailed off as the engine picked up rpm's driving towards 5903 Boulder Hwy to meet up with Tim.

With a height of over 6 feet 5 inches and weighing in at 340 pounds or so, Tim was a mountain of a man. His reddish shoulder length hair and missing teeth made him look more like a Hell's Angel member than a gun storeowner. When Glen and Mace arrived, the store was dark inside and it appeared Tim had closed up early. Perfect. Tim was a smart guy, and knew when he'd received the call that they'd need privacy. He told everyone he was closing early for a family emergency. He waited until the store had cleared, locked the door, and turned the sign from open to close. Once his two workers had punched out, Tim waited in his back office for Glen and Mace to arrive. Tim waited for the secret knock, then peeked through the peephole, and let them in.

The 3 buddies each shook hands and remarked about how long it had been since last seeing each other. Tim thanked them both again for saving his ass and received the standard, "It's cool man. Forget about it." "What do you guys need this time?" Tim asked. Mace pulled a list from his front shirt pocket and handed it to him. Tim whistled and said, "Man, I don't know who you guys are after, but I'm damn glad it ain't me!"

They quickly gathered the requested supplies and placed them in an olive green duffel bag. Mace asked Tim what the damage was and he replied, "Get outta here before I call the police and report a robbery." Then the big, burly man smiled, patted Mace on the back, and said the debt had already been paid. After thanking Tim, Mace and Glen hit the door and sped off in Glen's

Volkswagen to the warehouse where he kept his extra supply of electronic equipment.

The pair arrived at the fake meeting place they'd chosen earlier that afternoon. Appearances are the most crucial factors in games of this magnitude. The area had been scouted for escape routes and controlled entrances. It was almost perfect; there was only one way in and two ways out. The two exits had been fitted with metal plates that had spikes pointing at the tires. Travelling in the correct direction, the spikes folded down allowing a vehicle to proceed normally; however, a vehicle going the wrong way would have punctured tires, making this an extremely efficient system for deterring theft. The high ground wasn't a problem either because most of the buildings surrounding this warehouse were only one level. Their structure was situated several blocks from the main road and in the middle of a long row. Anyone trying to sneak up on this location would have a difficult time finding suitable cover for hiding. The parking lot was expansive to allow the large trucks to maneuver. This design left a large area of open territory that would be difficult to cross unseen. With the large, bright lights strategically located around each building; this seemed a daunting task at best. Would this turn into a shootout? Would this warehouse be ambushed? Would this turn out to be a wasted night with no one showing up? Who knew the answers? All they could do was to prepare for as many eventualities as possible.

Glen set up a couple of hidden cameras with speakers and scanned the area for any other electronic listening devices. He found none, so Mace arranged some mirrors and Plexiglas walls to create a temporary hallway. He wanted this setup to be very much like a maze; one in which he knew the path in and out and could use this to his fullest advantage if needed. The meeting room was set up with a table, four chairs, and a few surprises in case things turned sour. A smoke canister and a flash grenade were wired under the table. The chairs each concealed an extra pistol in case Mace was out of ammunition or lost his during a surprise counter attack.

If Mace was in agreement, Glen requested, "Hey, Mace. Let's try not to turn this into a blood bath if possible. Okay?"

Mace hadn't had to fire his gun in quite some time and inside he was just as concerned and cautious as Glen. They finished the assigned tasks, met back at the front door, and agreed that they had done a good job for such short notice. Next came the hard part: sitting and waiting to see who arrived and what transpired.

Mace checked his watch just as the sun was beginning to sink from sight. In about thirty minutes the lights around the compound would automatically illuminate the parking lot and the entrance area. All that would remain would be small pockets of darkness capable of concealing possible predators. Glen and Mace were equipped with night vision goggles and fully expected that someone would be using the shadows for camouflage. The minutes dragged on like hours and all remained quiet and still. As eleven thirty approached, they began wondering if this was going to come up dry. Now it was midnight and still nothing. Mace scanned the area with the infrared detector and picked up a small trace of a heat signature. It was too small to be a human being, but it was definitely moving in the direction of the warehouse in a slow and stealthy manner. Mace motioned to Glen as he was doing the same when a brilliant light emanated from the target. Apparently someone was there, and that bright light effectively rendered the night vision goggles useless. Mace quickly shed the goggles but continued to use the infrared scanner. Nothing else happened for nearly ten minutes, and their eyes readjusted to the night vision goggles they had donned again.

The time was around 12:35 when Mace finally saw a figure slinking along the warehouse wall toward the door. Once the shadowy silhouette entered the door, Glen and Mace drew their handguns and followed to see who it was. Easing through the entrance, Mace slipped the safety off, and he and Glen proceeded in standard two by two cover formation along the hallway that had been created. Upon arriving at the room with the table and chairs, they found Donald Roy Perkins, sitting calmly with a lit cigarette in one hand and a Glock 17 in the other. After 11 months and thousands of miles crisscrossing the US, Mace was finally face to face with his quarry.

Perkins lowered his gun and said, "I came as soon as I got your message, Mace. This site of yours appears to be clean, and I reconned the area before I came in. Careful, there's a smoke canister and a flash grenade under this table. I've taken the liberty of removing the pistols from under the chairs though. A wanted man can never be too careful. Right? Now, what's on your mind, Mace?"

What was on his mind was that Donald Roy was no ordinary skipper, and Mace began to wonder just how deep this rabbit hole went. Concealing his admiration for Donald Roy Perkins, Mace sat down, lowered his pistol, and earnestly began to study the man he'd spent all those long, hard, tiring months attempting to capture. Mace asked Donald what branch of the service he'd been in.

Donald replied that he was a former Army Ranger who had survived being captured behind enemy lines and had managed to escape. He'd made it back to base camp with vital intelligence of location, size, and strength of the enemy. His reward was being promoted to Captain and then being honorably discharged when his wife had unexpectedly gotten pregnant. Donald explained how he'd spent untold hours caring for his wife and daughter when Sara, his wife, was battling double pneumonia. He and Angela, Angel for short, would rock while Donald hummed and sang lullabies to her.

He no longer seemed to Mace to be this evil man who could've killed his wife and daughter; or it could be his Ranger training was even better than Mace had heard. Time alone would reveal which of these two was the truth.

"Let's get this started Mace; we may not have much time," Donald Roy said. "Besides you, someone else is on my trail, and I haven't as yet figured out whom that someone is or why they're after me. That's where you come in, I hope."

"Donald, I've come into possession of an audio tape that claims you are being framed and forced to remain silent," Mace said. "I'm not certain this tape is authentic or factual. Let's say the tape is real. What I need to know from you is have you been made aware of this? Tell me if you know why you are being framed for murdering your wife and daughter. Who has you on the run from prosecution for a crime you didn't commit? I can't solve this and clear your good name as long as you keep information from me. I'm trying to help you and keep my reputation in tact at the same time, so if you want my help, the time to speak up is now."

Donald took a deep drag off his cigarette, looked Mace in the eyes, and began to tell him of the events of that fateful night. It read like a horror movie. The assailants who awoke him wore masks and night vision goggles as they dragged him from his bed, so he had no idea what they looked like. He was forced to watch as his wife was repeatedly stabbed while she slept. Then the scene was repeated with his daughter. After both were dead, with a knife at his throat, his hands were dipped into their blood and fingerprints were left for the police. The intruders gave him a script to read and memorize for answering the questions from the police and his lawyer. Following their directions to the last letter, he soon discovered he had been sold down the river.

With arrangements made for his safe transport away from Las Vegas, credit cards and money had been set up for him to allow a fresh start in a new city. While awaiting transportation to the courthouse, he was slipped

a note telling him that if he didn't want to end up doing

time on death row until his execution date he should run

and run now…

"I see," Mace said. "So who has been providing

you with all of the information regarding me like the

times of my arrival and what I'm searching for?"

Donald Roy explained, "I receive a cell phone call

telling me to pick up a package at a particular place under

a fake name. Inside that package are a new cell phone

and the information on you and your progress regarding

my capture. I am also told to dispose of the old cell

phone or better yet, give it to some homeless person so

that if it's being tracked it will send the tracker in the

wrong direction."

Mace asked him if all of the packages looked alike and if he had kept any that could be examined for clues.

Donald replied, "Yes, but I don't have it with me; it's at my hideaway."

Mace suggested they depart the warehouse before receiving unwanted visitors and Donald agreed to allow Mace to ride with him while Glen followed them.

Riding beside Donald on the trip to his secret lair, Mace had a gut feeling that this night was really only beginning to reveal its true purpose. Was this a trap to ensnare him and Glen? Would he be able to glean any information from the alleged package? Did this package even exist? How was he going to solve this and discover who had really killed Donald's family and why? What if Donald had planned and executed this ruse for some as yet unknown reason. Mace's mind whirred with questions.

The house that Donald Roy Perkins brought them to was located in an upscale neighborhood not too far from the strip. It was dark and quiet except for the faint sound of a dog barking as they walked to the front door.

"Do you have a dog in there?" Mace inquired.

"No," Donald replied, "It's just a recording set to a motion sensor to keep kids and burglars away."

Mace suggested they wait a few minutes to allow him and Glen a chance to recon the yard area. Donald assured the two that he had taken care of all of those kinds of concerns before leaving for the meeting. Still, that gut feeling told Mace to recheck his efforts, and he wasn't going to be denied.

Mace slipped off around the left side and Glen went to the right. They slowly crept along the wall of the house passed the edge of the neighbor's fence and met up on the patio. Just as he was about to holster his weapon, the compressor for the air conditioner kicked on and Mace spun around ready to fire a couple of shots but caught himself before he actually pulled the trigger. Both he and Glen got a good laugh out of that and agreed the yard was clean and decided to go ahead inside.

"Geez, Mace! Are you a little bit jumpy or what?" Glen asked.

Mace replied, "I've never lost a draw down with one yet, Glen."

Donald Roy Perkins put the key in the lock, turned the handle, and swung open the door to reveal a house that had been hurriedly ransacked. All three of the men drew their weapons and performed a room-to-room search. Each yelled "clear" after sweeping each room in the house and finding it empty.

"Apparently, we must've just missed them or they heard us coming and left because they didn't finish searching the last two rooms of the house," Donald stated. Donald Roy went over to the upturned dresser in the master bedroom and righted it before stepping into the closet. He had placed the package under a false bottom in his suitcase.

Mace unzipped the luggage and found it there just as Donald had described. A thick manila envelope with red printed block letters on the front contained what appeared to be a dossier. Mace had seen enough of those in the Navy and working for judges on bail skippers to recognize it immediately. These dossiers are usually reserved for top-secret missions and contain more of private information than one would imagine. It could contain family's names and history, any trips taken recently, along with financial records. Many times, they also listed the names of dentists and doctors who had treated the person in question. A person's whole life could be viewed in one neat little file. This one had the name Mace Dugan on it.

Details of this type can usually be found when dealing with the CIA or the FBI or some other government entity. Mace felt his face get hot and red as the blood rushed into his cheeks. "What in the bloody hell is going on here?" he asked aloud. This case was feeling like he kept getting more questions than answers and no closer to a resolution.

Mace asked Donald Roy when he'd gotten this dossier and Donald said, "That was the first one I received." Donald had been using the information found in it to keep close tabs on Mace. "Are you having my team followed right now, Donald Roy, because we've noticed some counter- surveillance teams watching my office and staff?" Mace asked.

"Mace, I know you don't believe me, but I don't have a team. Someone else is in charge here," Donald replied. "What do you say we put our efforts together and see if we can figure out this whole mess?"

Mace grabbed the dossier and the envelope as Glen grabbed Donald Roy. They left the safe house and headed over to Glen's lab. Although Glen was a wizard with audio and video, what was needed now was a forensic specialist, and on Mace's team that person was Karla Reams.

Karla had always had a love for science and chemistry. Mace knew if anyone could gather evidence from that envelope and dossier it would be her, so he picked up his cell and gave her a call. She answered on the third ring with her usual sparkling personality and cheery voice, "Hey, what's up Mace?"

"Hey, Karla, I'm in need of some of your special skills. Are you available for a couple of hours?"

"Do I need to go get my kit, Mace?" Karla asked.

"Yes, Karla. I'll need you to bring your kit and your sharpest mental deductive reasoning. Meet us at Glen's lab as soon as you can. Okay?"

"Will do, Mace. Give me about three hours. I'll need to finish up here, and drive home and grab my crime kit before I get to Glen's place. Oh, and Mace, I'm gonna need some money up front for my efforts and supplies on this one. Got it? You still owe me from the last time, and while I always enjoy reviewing evidence, keep in mind that I don't get my supplies for free" Karla petitioned.

"Yeah, Karla, I got it," Mace answered. We'll have something for you the minute you arrive. I promise."

While waiting for Karla to arrive with her evidence collection kit, Mace, Donald Roy, and Glen sat around the table putting names and possible motives for the frame job onto a sheet of paper. They bounced ideas off each other and made an attempt not to discount anyone Donald had known on his jobs, acquaintances or neighbors with whom he had experienced disagreements. They put down every name Donald recalled and every motive from money to jealousy, envy, anger, or even spite. The result was nearly a full notebook page long and divided into two columns at its completion. They would use this list as a starting point when Karla finished her study of the dossier and envelope to cross check the names. Their hope was that one or more of the names would show up as having handled or come in contact with either piece of evidence. If that turned out to be false, they'd see if Karla could provide any new names to include on the list. Hopefully she would find fingerprints or trace evidence that could put them on the right track to finding the responsible party or parties for this heinous crime.

Mace got up from the table and went to the fridge looking for beer and a snack. After opening the door and peeking inside he looked back and asked if anyone else wanted anything. Just after he'd gotten a beer for himself and one for Glen, a knock came at the door. Glen opened the door and in stepped Karla with her trusty briefcase.

"Hey, girl. We've got you all set up over here on this table," Mace said as he directed her to it. "Sounds good, Mace. By the way, have you got my money?" Mace laughed and handed her a stack of bills he'd put in a brown paper bag and told her it was her lunch money. She took the bag, smiled, and headed immediately to the table, slipped on her rubber gloves, and began to examine the envelope first.

Karla was a really sweet, kind hearted, raven-haired beauty with bright green eyes. She had spent time on the Las Vegas Crime Unit but decided that the bureaucratic red tape and ridiculous rules of evidence chain was just too much for her to contend with on a daily basis. She stood about 5 feet 3 inches tall, and though she had a really nice body, she hid it under loose fitting clothes and an oversized white lab coat. Mace had contacted her to join the team after watching her testify in a case that no one wanted because of the high profile nature of the deceased. She amazed him with her ability to tell a tale and paint a picture from the evidence she'd examined. When she spoke about the details and facts she had tested to prove her theory, the images came alive for her listeners. From that first chance meeting, he had made it his responsibility to keep close tabs on her whereabouts. If she were to leave the Crime Unit or get a promotion, Mace wanted to know about it. That's exactly what happened.

After resigning, she went on the lecture circuit. Mace contacted her about doing some contract work for the agency in her spare time. Later she had told him that she wasn't going to consider it originally. However, after they'd met, she had changed her mind and the two had become pretty close friends. Mace had helped her with some trouble she had had with a stalker, so she felt indebted to him and consequently had agreed to help find the locations of several jumpers. Together they had decided that whenever the need arose, they'd always be there for each other. Mace knew if there was anything at all to be found on either piece of evidence, Karla could find it. He was counting on it. Karla always got a very stern and serious glare on her face when studying evidence and she simply would not tolerate being hurried. To say she was a methodical perfectionist would have been an understatement, but that's what made her so good at her chosen profession.

Time crawled along during Karla's painstakingly slow but thorough examination. Mace paced the floor and tried to remain calm and aloof, not wanting to interfere. Glen had kicked off his shoes and was napping on the sofa while Donald Roy was quietly staring at the pictures of his wife and daughter he carried in his wallet.

Mace ambled over to take a look at Donald Roy's pictures and saw tears were rolling out of his eyes and down his cheeks as he sobbed in complete silence. After seeing this, Mace decided to leave him alone and allow him his solace. These didn't seem to Mace to be the emotions of a man who had brutally stabbed his wife and daughter to death in calculated fashion. Mace's cold, stubborn heart was beginning to warm to the idea that this man was innocent and that he and the team had to do everything humanly possible to right this wrong.

Mace wandered into the kitchen wanting to make a fresh pot of coffee. It took some digging around in several cabinets before he found an unopened can of Maxwell House Breakfast Blend Medium Roast. Whenever he needed to collect his thoughts or do introspective study, he'd discovered that a steaming hot cup of coffee could be very soothing. Was there some therapeutic property inside the java bean? Regardless of

the answer, this simple treat was just the little extra in his

life that allowed him some comfort inside while chaos

surrounded him. Sipping on the second cup and nibbling

on a cinnamon biscotti stick from Glen's cookie jar, Mace

drifted into a state of semi-consciousness. A loud voice in

the other room startled him back to reality.

Mace jumped up from the table and dashed over

to where the jubilant sound emanated to see what was

happening.

Karla was standing with a huge grin on her face

and waving a piece of paper in the air. "Mace, this may

be the only thing we recover from this case, but I believe

it'll be significant," she said emphatically. "Come look at

this and tell me what you see." Karla passed him the

paper and he suddenly felt that twang in the pit of his

stomach. Surely what he saw there was some kind of

mistake. What else could explain the fact that there was a latent image of writing spelling out, "Go to The Safe House in Milwaukee and seek out your next contact"?

The name of the contact was smeared and wrinkled, and Karla said she had tried several different solutions to reveal its identity, but with no success. She suggested they go to Milwaukee and search for additional clues with the help of Donald Roy Perkins. This case was turning out to be exactly like most cases had been in the past. Somewhere along the way, the spot from which the case cracking evidence would eventually come had already been explored. The time had come to inform the crew that they needed to catch a flight up north, and they'd better dress warmly if they wanted to enjoy this trip.

The team gathered in a circle around Mace at the table and began to formulate a plan. "I'll call Tonya and have her check on available flight times for departure," Mace said. She can also book reservations for two adjoining rooms at a hotel. "Glen, you and Donald Roy need to pack anything we can't get by security at the airport. We'll need to box it and have it shipped to the Safe House for us to use after we arrive. I'll call Linda or Mark to let them know that the package is coming and have one of them set it aside for me. We need a map of the Milwaukee area so I can show all of you where the Safe House is located. Let's synchronize our watches, and we'll meet back here at 0900 with updates. If anyone encounters any difficulty, call me immediately on my cell. Preparing in advance may give us the upper hand we need should we encounter any resistance," Mace said.

Karla was ready to head for home, so Mace caught a ride with her while Glen agreed to stick with Donald Roy until boarding the plane. Mace stepped outside, smiled and remarked what a fantastic team the group made. Karla concurred and said that she had always wanted to go to a spy bar and see what it was like to be Mace Dugan for a little while. She hit the door lock on her key fob, and they settled into her slate blue Audi TT as the top began to open and the engine roared to life. "Man, this is some sweet ride you have here, Karla," Mace told her. "Looks like the lecture circuit pays better than I thought it did. Maybe there's a need for an ex-Navy intelligence officer to explain the finer techniques of skip tracing and bounty hunting."

She smiled wryly and said sarcastically, "If only we knew somebody with those talents, there just might be." Karla stepped on the gas and left tire tracks on the pavement as she left Glen's road and headed towards Mace's condo. This little convertible had some serious power, and Mace was slightly surprised at the way it seemed to change Karla's demeanor. She weaved and dodged her way through traffic like she was on the autobahn. His neck jerked as Karla whipped into the parking lot and brought the car to a rapid halt with a jolt. Mace unbuckled his seat belt, thanked Karla for the lift, and turned to go inside. Squealing tires told him Karla had just pulled out, and he said a quick prayer for her safety, before closing his door.

Flipping on the light switch, he saw the dirty clothes still piled near the washer. "Damn, I see the laundry fairy passed over my condo again," Mace thought to himself. If he didn't want to buy a whole new wardrobe, he was going to have to make time to handle that chore. He separated them into small stacks of like items as he'd been taught and turned the dial to heavy dirt. "Mom would be so proud of me if she could see me doing it just like she had," he said. As the water began rising, Mace went about the task of emptying the pockets. The little slip of paper with Amber's phone number was still neatly folded inside one of them. After he opened it, he decided to toss it into the trash basket like so many others he had been handed over the years.

The voice mail for Tonya came on the phone and he left instructions for her to call him when she could. No sense in leaving a long message for her to have to interpret when they could speak instead. Her skill in taking care of these mundane duties so quickly and efficiently was the reason he paid her so well, and she knew it. When he had first hired her she wasn't always reliable, but after a discussion with her, she had blossomed into an asset and vital member of the team. Mace knew Tonya would have little trouble handling these tasks, so he went about packing for the return trip to the frozen north.

Thoughts of Linda entered his mind he started to call and alert her that he'd be returning soon. Several weeks had passed since their goodbye at the terminal gate, and he found himself remembering the smell of her perfume. Lying on the bed and closing his eyes, he allowed his mind to relive the time they had spent together. Her friendly personality and the way she made him feel made him think the cold weather might not be too bad after all. Talking with her was so easy. Their conversations flowed in a way that he'd never experienced with any other woman. They shared a special connection or bond. He had always been about the conquest before, just using women to escape the cold dead feeling he usually felt in the deep recesses of his heart. But they seemed to have more than a few things in common; her intelligence, drive, and purpose mirrored his pretty closely. If there was a chance for him to get to know more about her, he didn't want to let it slip away.

The washer cycle finished, and it dawned on him he'd been lying there about thirty minutes thinking about her. Only three more loads to go before he would be finished. "I'll call Linda after I have more information," he decided as he started the next wash load and transferred the first grouping into the dryer.

Mace headed to the gym for a quick workout in an effort to help clear his mind of this case for a short time. Building up a good sweat by lifting weights allowed for the body's natural rejuvenation. With the washer and dryer going, he could get in some cardio and a few reps of curls for the old biceps before needing to be back home. Ever since his boot camp days, he'd found it helped him gain a certain mental acuity while knocking out pushups, sit-ups, and chin-ups. As part of the condo complex, they had a place on the fifth floor that provided the tenants its use for this purpose.

Choosing to run up the three flights of stairs from his room to the gym was normally how he got there. Since he hadn't been regularly exercising in quite a while, his heart started beating rapidly in his chest. His breathing was quick, and he was already beginning to form sweat beads on his forehead. "You'd better get back in shape and lay off the vanilla lattes for a while, old boy," he told himself. "If three flights of stairs will do this to you, you had better pray you don't have to chase anyone." Mace calmed himself before exiting the stairwell and entering the gym.

The forty-pound dumbbells fit easily into his palms and he sat on a bench and watched his form in the mirror. After ten reps on each arm, he increased ten pounds. He repeated this, and then went up to the sixty pounders. Not wanting to overdo and risk injury, he stopped at that weight. With 225 pounds on the bar, Mace completed a set of eight lifts, three times on the bench press. Next, he alternated between sit-ups, pushups, and chin-ups maxing out with each one. A short run on the treadmill completed the regimen and he noticed he'd been gone almost an hour and prepared to return to the condo.

Tonya had called while he was out and left a message for him to call her back. Getting her on the phone, he gave her the information for the team. "When do you need the details, Mace?" asked Tonya. Mace replied, "We are meeting tomorrow morning at nine, so any time between now and then will be fine." She assured him that he'd get her call before that meeting took place.

"You truly are the best, Tonya," Mace told her. "I don't know what I'd do without you".

As Mace stood in the hot shower, he remembered that he needed to call both Glen and Linda before turning in for the night. He dried off, slipped on a robe, and grabbed the phone. First to get his call was Linda. Mace wanted to alert her that he would be returning soon and that he'd give her another call when he had the itinerary. "Be on the lookout for a package I'm sending to the Safe House, and set it aside for me, please," Mace requested.

Linda agreed adding she was very glad to hear from him and would be looking forward to seeing him again soon. Next, Mace dialed Glen to suggest an idea. Mace told him that before they left Las Vegas they should leak false information to several local loudmouths. "Let's report that we found evidence that is going to blow the lid completely off of this conspiracy against Donald Roy Perkins and expose the real culprit once and for all," Mace suggested.

Glen agreed that he liked the idea and would take care of the particulars. "Get some rest, and I'll see you tomorrow, Mace", said Glen. After hanging up the phone, Mace turned down the covers, slipped into bed, and closed his eyes.

It paid to have friends who knew better than to ask questions sometimes. Such was the case with the package that needed to be delivered to the Safe House. A contact Mace had made earlier in his career was just such a friend. His name was Andrew or Andy to his friends. Andy's official line of work was providing hot-shot service overnight from point A to point B with minimal fuss. Upon rising the next morning, the first thing Mace did was touch base with Andy. Telling him of the need for his service, Mace advised that he'd call Andy back to let him know the pickup and drop-off locations. Experience had taught him to always pay back favors done for him, so Andy was more than willing to oblige.

Everyone was already at the meeting when Mace arrived. Tonya had just given him the details of the trip, and after a brief discussion, they all headed for the airport. On the flight back to Milwaukee Mace couldn't fight off the feeling that he was being toyed with like a yo-yo. Someone else had the string, pulling him in any direction they wanted. As a Scorpio, this didn't sit well with Mace. He was much more accustomed to being the one in control than being controlled. He didn't adjust well to someone else being in control of his actions. As he pondered his situation it begun to stir some anger inside of him, the kind of anger that burns deep down inside and feeds the drive to overcome current circumstances. The time had come to quit playing along and do something totally out of character to shake things up a bit and become less predictable. Someone out there had studied his tactics and personality and they had Mace dancing to their tune, which was going to change because he was about to react out of character. Mace decided to do the exact opposite of what he'd normally do to see if he couldn't force their hand and maybe cause a slip up by whoever had been jerking his string. Surely this would upset the plans of the yo-yo master and force them into playing the game differently.

Upon arriving in the Milwaukee airport everyone expected Mace to want to head straight over to The Safe House. He sent Karla, Glen, and Donald Roy Perkins to the hotel to await further instructions. When Linda answered the phone, he told her that after he'd gotten back to Las Vegas he began to miss her, and that once he arrived in town he wanted to drive straight to her house and see her. She told him she was in the middle of a business meeting at home that should conclude in several hours but would be free afterward. Mace lied and told her that he was still in flight, and by the time he arrived, got the luggage and a rental car, it would more than likely be three or so hours from then anyway. She believed him, and they hung up the phone. Mace sped over to her neighborhood to see who was in attendance at this meeting being held in her mansion. No one was above suspicion at this point, and it was time for a little recon work.

One benefit of being nice to people was that they usually didn't mind helping you out or bending a few rules when you tell them you are trying to surprise someone they had seen you with before. That was the tactic Mace used on the security guard at the entrance to Linda's neighborhood when he pulled up and was stopped.

"Hey, John, it's me Mace, that friend of Linda's that stayed with her at her house a little while back. How are you doing today?" Mace asked.

John replied, "It sure was cold and windy that day, too." They chatted for a few more minutes and then Mace asked him about letting him slip through to surprise Linda.

John shrugged and mumbled something about rules; then he said, "Sure, Mace. Good luck with Miss Linda. You two were quite the couple, you know?"

"Yeah I know, and thank you, John," was Mace's reply. "Stay warm, buddy, and stay out of this wind if you can."

The gate lifted and off Mace drove toward Linda's house, but he paused to park a few driveways before hers. There were three cars he could see in the driveway and who knew if anyone had parked in the garage. Patiently he waited in the cold to catch a glimpse of the attendees at this gathering. Mace was getting that feeling in his gut that something was about to happen. The snow crunched beneath his black combat boots as he made his way closer to the house using the cover of the gazebo and the trees. A thick scarf was covering his face so that his breathing wouldn't give him away. The meeting participants were hard to make out through the monocular he held to his right eye. His attempt to gather useful information from this meeting was becoming less and less likely as his toes became more and more frigid. Mace decided to check out the contents of the autos in the driveway to see if they held any valuable clues.

The last car held a manila envelope that could be a dossier, but it could just as easily not be. It was beginning to look more and more like he'd have to wait until he could see Linda face to face to determine if she was part of any nefarious plot involving him and Donald Roy Perkins or if she, too, was only an unwitting participant in this elaborate charade.

Mace made his way back to the car and decided to wait patiently until Linda's meeting finished and everyone had left. It was only about another 30 minutes according to their earlier phone conversation, so he moved his rental car farther away to avoid being seen sitting in it when the meeting adjourned. Mace jotted down a few notes and observations he'd made while watching the activity at Linda's house in a trusty notebook he kept and reviewed the facts currently known in this case. Usually he'd review the notebook's contents alone several times during a case. This time he was so caught up in the knots of lies and the romance that he hadn't taken the time until now. He reviewed the statements of each of the people he'd interviewed at The Safe House as a refresher. When he met with them again later that night, he wanted to be familiar with their statements so he could see who might be lying.

Chapter Four

Misdirection

Mace had just completed reading the statements and events from The Safe House workers when it began to snow. Although he was from Las Vegas and really loved the warm temperatures and low humidity, he'd discovered he really enjoyed watching the snow fall. There was a certain serenity to be found in this act of nature. In a trancelike state, he watched each flake waft its way from the sky to the ground, blending with the other falling flakes to form a luminous blanket that covered everything. It was at that moment that a car horn startled him and snapped him back to reality from the meditation.

It seems he'd picked a house on Linda's block that was receiving a package from UPS, and it was that horn he'd just heard. He slowly backed out of the driveway and noticed that the meeting at Linda's house was ending, so he decided to pull in and park. Just as he got out of the rental car and began walking toward Linda's front door, the garage door opened. Linda stood inside with open arms and a huge smile. She ran to Mace, jumped into his arms, and said, "Mace, I'm so glad you came back to see me so soon." He hugged her and they kissed. She was wearing a tan dress and her hair fell loosely around her shoulders. She smelled of wild flowers and coconuts. After Mace hugged her tightly for a few seconds, he told her that this trip was business as well as pleasure.

"It seems there must be additional clues or information here, so my team and I came as quickly as we could. How was your meeting?" he asked.

"Oh, the usual stuff," she said. "Someone was upset because someone didn't show up for their shift, so we had to discuss options of reprimanding or firing them. Then we had a financial report and some new ideas for promotions to help increase profits. I don't want to talk about that stuff though, I'd rather hear about your flight and how long you're staying. Do you have reservations with a hotel for you and your team? You could always have the man room again," she purred as she winked and squeezed his arm.

Mace pinched Linda's butt while gazing into her eyes and said, "I need a cup of coffee and to touch base with the team. Then we can enjoy some together time, and I'll catch you up on your curiosity."

Linda and Mace made their way into the house and down the hall to the kitchen for some coffee. Linda put the water in the pot, added the coffee grounds, and flipped the switch. Mace sidled up to a bar stool and watched her remembering the last time they had made love. Mace had never given his heart completely to anyone, but Linda made him want to give up the bachelor days and actually think about settling down.

Linda turned and caught him staring as she reached for the cups in the cabinet. Slowly she turned to face him. Flashing her sparkling smile, she asked, "Are you sure it's coffee you want, Mace?" He glanced at his watch and quickly figured they had time for some bedroom activity if it didn't take too long. She answered her own question by dropping her dress to the floor, slipping off her heels, and racing up the stairs, giggling all the way, and taunting him to catch her.

Topping the stairs, he saw her posing at the doorway with one leg teasingly hooked around the frame and one hand's index finger beckoning him to come join her. She seductively whispered, "Come and get me, big boy, if you're man enough." Mace stepped through the doorway and found her completely nude, gazing at him with a wanton expression and slightly parted red lips. He grabbed her and kissed her deeply. Their tongues played in each other's mouths before he gently bit her lower lip causing her to moan. She peeled off his shirt as he released his belt and began to unlace his boots. Linda took his hand in hers and led Mace to her bed. They fell onto the comforter and he caressed every inch of her body while kissing her neck, shoulders, and nibbling on the lobe of her right ear. "My God, she is the most beautiful woman I've ever put my hands on," he thought to himself. They kissed, fondled, and made love for a while before falling fast asleep holding each other.

The alarm on Mace's watch rang in his ear awakening him from a restful sleep. Linda was snuggled up next to him and appeared contented as he watched her breathing and sleeping. Slowly he eased himself from the bed so as not to disturb her, but she awoke anyway. He suggested a quick shower and a change of clothes before they headed over to The Safe House. She readily agreed and they slipped into the shower to scrub each other. Mace truly didn't know what he was going to do if Linda was somehow involved in this whole conspiracy to frame Donald Roy Perkins. As she washed his back and he scrubbed hers, she sensed something was going through Mace's head that was causing a change in his mood.

She asked him what he was thinking about and if she could help with whatever uneasy thoughts he had running around in his head. He told her that some things didn't jive with this case and that he was working through some of the details and inconsistencies in his mind. She suggested he try what she did when some problem was bothering her: write it down on paper strips one sentence at a time. This allows for rethinking the order in which things may have occurred; then each strip can be put into order.

Mace decided to give this idea a try when they made it to her office, and he thanked her for the suggestion. They finished dressing and then went back to the kitchen to make some fresh coffee. The first pot was cold, and Linda tossed it out in the sink. It was still very cold outside; snow was continuing to fall, and it showed no signs of letting up any time soon. They filled a couple of thermos bottles and headed for the door to the garage. Linda suggested they ride together and let her drive since she was accustomed to the slick, snow-covered roads. Mace got into the passenger seat of her Mercedes and buckled up for the trip to the Safe House.

Linda raised the garage door, backed down the driveway, and drove off towards the Safe House as it closed. He sipped on the coffee as she turned on the seat warmers and the radio played an Eagles tune. They both sang along to "Seven Bridges Road." Sometimes songs come on the radio that seems to fit the moment in time that is occurring. This Eagles song was falling into that category, except instead of giving up a musical career, Mace would be giving up a life of bad road food and cheap hotels. The snow hitting the windshield made a rhythmic sound and the wind worked to move her car as it blew. Linda's ability to maintain control in this type of storm was impressive. It was easy to see that she had years of experience with these kind of conditions.

They discussed what might be found as far as evidence to exonerate Donald Roy Perkins and what the purpose of framing him was. Was it a jilted lover or a jealous colleague? Could it be an angry ex, or had he somehow seen or gained knowledge of something he wasn't supposed to? Linda helped Mace run through several scenarios each explaining the possibilities from their own perspectives. She reminded Mace that they screened all potential employees for the Safe House and performed background checks as well as random drug screenings. It would be difficult to imagine anyone in her employ killing Donald Roy Perkins' family then framing and blackmailing him. Almost all of the workers at the Safe House were 25 or younger, so if it were one of them, there would almost certainly have to be accomplices Linda reasoned. At 45 years of age, it didn't make sense that Donald Roy could have crossed someone from the

Safe House badly enough to warrant them murdering his family. It was a most perplexing case indeed.

Linda turned the car into the private parking garage and pulled into her reserved spot. She leaned over and kissed Mace before they exited the car. Looking into his eyes, she said she thought that she could feel herself falling for him. They huddled closely together holding hands as they walked to the special entrance. Mace wondered what his team had found while he had been enjoying Linda's company and her...hospitality.

They arrived at Linda's office and found no one there. After walking to the surveillance room to check the cameras, they tried to locate Mace's team. The crowd inside began to build as darkness once again enveloped the city streets of Milwaukee. Linda and Mace decided to go downstairs and find her night manager Mark to see if he knew where the team might be. As they turned to leave the room Linda saw Mark standing in the doorway with an odd expression on his face. Linda asked if he was feeling all right, and he held up a bloody hand as he began to pass out. Mace rushed over, caught him, and lowered him to the ground.

"Mark, what happened?" he asked. "How did you get hurt?" His eyes were quickly sinking into his head, and Mace knew it wouldn't be long before he slipped into shock. Mark mumbled something about standing at his post down stairs and then feeling a sharp pain in his left lower back. He went on to say that he turned to see who had stabbed him and got a glimpse of someone in black high heels, stockings, and a short skirt before they blended into the crowd.

Mace told him to stop talking and to rest quietly while they got him some first aid. Mark nodded that he understood. Mace told Linda to grab something he could use as a bandage while they elevated his feet and tried to make him comfortable.

Linda was grabbing for her cell phone to call 911 as she searched for bandages. Mace could hear her giving the address as her voice trailed off down the hall. She returned with a small first aid kit and a tablecloth, which he ripped into strips and made a nice square to cover the puncture wound in Mark's back. The tiny kit had precious little in the way of salve or ointment, and Mace was praying for some sulfa powder. Finding only Neosporin, he dressed the wound quickly and placed heavy pressure against Mark's back. Mace then tied the strips around Mark's waist as tightly as he could until he feared possible tissue damage from lack of blood and oxygen. Mark winced when Mace pulled the strips and indicating he was still hanging in there. All they could do now was to wait for the ambulance to arrive and pray that the patch job was good enough. One good thing was that the amount of blood seeping through the bandage onto the floor appeared to be lessening. The dispatcher was still on the phone with Linda and told her that the ambulance was two minutes out.

Now, there were even more questions to answer. Who stabbed Mark and why? "Were they hoping to kill him or just slow down my team and me? And where was that damned ambulance?" Mace wondered.

The paramedics arrived and quickly administered an IV line to keep Mark's fluid levels up while assessing his situation. Vital signs appeared to be in an acceptable range for his condition. His pulse was good and his blood pressure was slightly below normal, but if they could get him to the hospital quickly, the prognosis for recovery looked pretty good. Linda told Mace that Mark was her most trusted employee. They had been friends since their college days, and he had promised to always be there for her and he had. Now his life could be hanging by a thread, so she was going to follow the ambulance to St. Joseph Hospital and wait for word on his condition after surgery.

As Mace realized just how fragile and fleeting life could truly be, he kissed Linda goodbye. She turned from their embrace and ran toward the gurney as the paramedics pushed Mark toward the service elevator, her high heels clicking on the polished floor as she disappeared from sight.

Mace decided to review the videotapes to see if he could find where Mark was when he was stabbed or to where his team had disappeared. He turned from the door where Linda had just left and he slumped down into a chair and began to roll back the tape of the bar area where Mark normally stood guard and greeted patrons.

The thought occurred that it would be a good idea to close and lock the door behind him so no one could sneak up and catch him unaware. He closed the door, turned the lock, and returned to the chair as the tape machine was whirring in fast motion reverse. The images on the screen appeared almost cartoon-like at that speed and were totally unrecognizable. Mace flipped the switch on the machine to normal speed forward and the bar came into focus. It was a very thin crowd with only three people sitting at the bar. Several couples were mingling around the tables, and the waitresses were easily moving and taking orders, but Mace didn't see Mark anywhere.

Time seemed to move at a snail's pace on the tape until Mace finally saw Mark walk by the lens and head over to the bar to greet Jamie, the bartender for the night. Jamie turned and poured a bottle of water into a mixed drink glass and handed it to him. Mark then paused and greeted each of the three guests seated at the bar making small talk before heading over to his normal perch. After fifteen minutes passed, the room began to grow more crowded. Mark was standing there watching the club as he normally did when the team walked up to him and they began talking. Mark nodded and pointed towards the hidden room. Karla, Glen and Donald Roy moved in that direction making their way through the crowd. Ten more minutes elapsed according to the counter on the camera screen before anyone else came into contact with Mark.

An average looking woman wearing a mini dress with huge flowers and a big bow approached Mark, and his facial expression changed to one of concern. She pointed towards the phone booth area and then back to Mark before walking away. He went over to the bar and handed Jamie his glass. They spoke for a few seconds as

Jamie leaned in towards him. As Mark turned to walk to

the phone booth, someone from the crowd bumped into

him. He reached for his back and pulled back a bloody

hand. Mace rewound the tape and reviewed it several

times but couldn't get a clear view of who had actually

stabbed Mark or the type of weapon used. He stumbled

as he turned around and looked straight at some woman

wearing all black before she disappeared into the crowd.

The rest of the tape only showed patrons laughing,

drinking, and having a good time.

Mace switched the camera viewer to the feed

from the hidden room to try to locate his team. The angle

of the camera was once again pointing towards the floor,

so he decided to go down and inspect the area himself.

He walked down the hall to the stairs and then down onto

the floor where the music and noise from the crowd was

loud and distracting. Mace paused at the bar to check

with Jamie to see if she had witnessed anything regarding Mark's attack. She stated she had just gone to the back room to get more vodka and noticed Mark wasn't at his post when she returned. She assumed he'd been called upstairs to meet with Linda but knew of no problem until later when Darla, one of the waitresses, passed by and told her about the incident.

Mace thanked her and headed for the hidden room. Something raised the hairs on the back of his neck as he approached, so he drew his pistol, slipped off the safety and pressed on the secret button and the door slowly opened. Once opened Mace stepped inside and found his team. Karla's hands had been bound behind her back and a gag placed in her mouth. She was still unconscious lying on her side and he began to remove her restraints. Her evidence case had been ransacked and remained scattered on the floor around her body. Glen had taken a nasty blow to the back of the head and was just beginning to regain consciousness. Glen rubbed his neck and turned his head to see Mace through bleary eyes. He asked Mace if everyone was okay. Donald Roy had been left conscious.

"What happened here tonight? Who did this to my team and Mark?" Mace wondered. "And how close are we to solving this case? Why had Donald Roy been left unharmed and aware"? He had to get the team back on their feet and feeling normal again before he was going to get any answers.

Mace gathered the contents of Karla's evidence case from the floor where she lay. She, Donald Roy, Glen, and Mace headed upstairs to the media room for some coffee and a briefing. As they talked about the events of that fateful night, the puzzle began to come into focus for Mace. Karla had gone into the hidden room first and was met by a chloroform rag to her face quickly rendering her immobile. Glen then thought he heard a scuffle, so he poked his head in to check on her and was hit over the head and knocked out. Donald Roy quickly followed but was grabbed immediately and held. He was questioned as to Mace's whereabouts, and the progress the team had made regarding his case. He was threatened to remain silent or end up dead instead of being imprisoned. Mace asked Donald Roy if he knew who his interrogator was. Donald Roy shook his head no, but he did say that it was a female who told him he was going to end up just like Mark.

After what Donald Roy said seemed like 10 or 15 minutes of questioning, he was told to turn around and face the wall. He feared he was about to be killed, but instead he felt a pain shoot through his head and the lights go black. "What happened to Mark?" Donald Roy asked.

"He was stabbed in the back. He's headed right now to St. Joseph Hospital in the back of an ambulance," Mace replied.

Mace suggested that Karla inspect her evidence case to see if there was anything in it that she had gathered prior to the attack that might be useful. She emptied her case onto the table and suddenly perked up when she found a rag that didn't belong to her. After slipping on some gloves, she took her tweezers and opened an evidence bag. She picked up the rag with the tweezers and sniffed it. "Eureka!" she shouted. "Mace, this is the rag that was used on me. It still smells of chloroform. Maybe, just maybe, if we're lucky there is some DNA or trace evidence on here that will help us locate who attacked us."

Mace asked Karla what she was going to compare

it to. "All of the items were removed from your

case during the attack, right?" asked Mace.

"Not so, Mace," she said. "I used my new

case when I was gathering the evidence of the

employees for exclusionary purposes and this is

my old one."

"Something tells me that it has to be an

employee," Mace said, "because of the familiarity

with

the layout of the club and the way they were able to

simply disappear so easily into the crowd. Karla, where's

your new case?"

She smiled and said she had put it in the

trunk of the rental car outside. Mace suggested

that they get the other case and find somewhere

to test this evidence and his theory. Everyone

agreed on the game plan and decided they should

return to the hotel room to rest up a little and

then get to work untangling this mystery. Karla

said she felt that if one person stood guard she

could probably work her magic throughout the

remainder of the night. Mace took the keys and

decided it would be best if drove while the others

took it easy with ice packs on their heads. They

were all beginning to feel a little bit better about

this trip and the case as they made their way to

the garage where Glen had parked the car. Mace

drew his gun again, walked to the trunk and

scanned the area to be certain no one was

waiting in ambush. Certain the coast was clear, he

popped open the trunk. There nestled right next

to the spare tire, snow chains and a flare kit, sat Karla's new evidence case.

Mace closed the trunk, got everyone inside, then started the engine and began the trek through the snow-covered streets to the hotel. A sense of calm was beginning to overtake him as Mace realized that the events of this day could have gone much worse. He was thankful that no one on the team was seriously injured. It was days like this that made him reconsider some of the choices he'd made with his life. He wondered if using good friends in dangerous business situations was such a good idea. The snow sloshed under the car tires, and by the time Mace turned into the parking lot of the hotel, all of his team, except Karla, was peacefully sleeping.

Good thing they had gotten two adjoining rooms at the hotel. Karla and Mace helped the guys from the car into the beds in the first room. After Mace placed the "Do Not Disturb" sign on the handle, and secured the door guard and lock, he joined Karla in the other room. Mace stood guard over the area while she began measuring, mixing, and spraying chemicals all over the rag, which she had cut into multiple squares. She had machines humming, whirring, and buzzing in a cacophony of sounds that made it extremely difficult for Mace to stay awake. If it weren't for several tricks he'd learned while serving in the navy, he too would have been sound asleep in no time flat. Mace called upon those hours of training and found himself becoming more alert.

His hearing became more acute, his eyesight ever keener.

Karla's eyes caught his, and she offered a wry smile as he appeared to her to be daydreaming. The truth was that he was actually recalling how many times these techniques he had found so mundane during his training regimen had served him well. Mace's reflexes and senses had been honed to such an alert state that he could even hear the low chime of the elevator as it passed their floor even though they were on the opposite side of the hotel. As the hours slipped by, Karla began to get frustrated. The clock was nearing 6 a.m. and she had exhausted almost every square she had cut from the rag. The faint sounds of snoring and breathing from the adjoining room changed pattern, and Mace knew that Donald Roy and Glen would soon be stirring.

Karla suggested that they wake the guys and take a break. "Remember, sometimes after a short break you can clear your head and see things better," she said.

Mace agreed with her, "I sure could use a hot cup of coffee and some breakfast." So with that as their motivation, they peeked in to see Glen and Donald Roy both rubbing their eyes and struggling to wake up. When breakfast and coffee was mentioned, the two of them shot out of bed as if it were on fire. Mace and Karla chuckled. After each had quickly freshened up, they opened the door and headed for the restaurant in the parking lot.

Although Mace was hungry, his thoughts were more on the condition of Mark after surgery at the hospital. He decided to give Linda another hour before calling her cell in case she was sleeping after a long night in the waiting room or by Mark's bedside.

The restaurant was nearly empty so finding a table was no problem. The hostess motioned for them to pick a spot anywhere they wanted saying she would send a waitress right over. They found a corner table so Mace could watch the exits. Jan, a bubbly brunette who was just a little too chipper this morning for the four of them, came over and began to spout off the specials. Mace politely interrupted her saying, "I'll have coffee, medium sweet with cream, and the buffet along with a tall glass of orange juice, please." Karla, Glen, and Donald Roy all decided Mace's choice was a good one and ordered the same. Jan wrote it down on her pad, then placed the pen above her right ear, smiled and said that she'd be right back with their coffee and orange juice. They rose from the table and charged the buffet like they hadn't eaten in a week. Mace piled scrambled eggs, bacon, hash browns,

blueberry muffins, and French toast sticks on his plate.

Afraid that the plate might not survive the trip back to the

table, he moved cautiously. The coffee was excellent and

Mace slammed down several cups, as did the others.

Poor Jan must've brought over three pots of coffee before

they finally began to feel their appetites subside. When

the bill arrived, each threw $15.00 on the table for an

$8.99 meal. They felt sure Jan would be appreciative of

the tip regardless of the mess and the constant trips to

the kitchen that she had endured.

As they walked back to the room, Mace's iPhone

began to vibrate with an incoming call from Linda. He

entered the security code for his phone and answered

"Good morning, Linda. How are you today?"

She chuckled softly and replied, "Very tired, but

working on awakening myself." She mentioned she was

sipping on a latte from Starbucks and chowing down on a scone reminiscent of their first meeting at the deli. Then Mace explained to her that they had all just finished eating as well and were on their way back to the room to complete the analysis of the rag Karla had found at the club. Mace inquired as to the current situation with Mark. She said that he had made it through surgery last evening and spent an uneventful night in the Intensive Care Unit. The plan for today was to keep him there for further observation and then move him into a private room for continued recovery. He had lost a significant amount of blood and would need a minimum of four days to regain his strength, but he should be awake periodically. Visiting would be allowed after he had been moved to his room. Her plans were to stay there and comfort him with a familiar face. Linda was feeling somehow guilty for the predicament her friend found himself facing. Mace tried to allay her worries and quickly realized it was a vain effort. They arrived at the door to the room and he told Linda to keep her chin up before he said goodbye. She said she would call him if anything changed. Mace decided that Linda already had more than enough on her plate so he's fill her in on the attack of his team later.

Mace pulled the card key from his pants pocket. After entering, they made their way over to the Karla's makeshift lab. Now refreshed from breakfast, she returned to her efforts with the last three squares of the chloroform rag. Mace was certain that Karla would be able to find something significant. After she finished testing her last sample, she reluctantly spilled the news that she had come up empty. She feared she had let them all down and dejectedly left the room.

Sometimes that which appears as a failure is actually a different measurement of success. Mace's dad had told this to him when he was just a young lad learning life's lessons through sports. He walked over to the rags and began to piece them back together like a jigsaw puzzle. After reassembling the scraps, he noticed a small letter near the edge of the fabric. Excitedly he called out for Karla to come and see if what he thought he saw was actually there or just wishful thinking. She almost knocked him over with a hug after she verified it was indeed what appeared to be a faded monogram. "Oh Mace," she said. "How did I miss that?" They now had a new direction to pursue feeling certain the letter was sure to match one of the employee's names. Whether it was the first or last would require the running of their list against Linda's employee database to narrow the suspects.

With the new evidence in tow, they were anxious to get

to the Safe House and access Linda's computer to begin

running the program and finding out how many of her

employees fit the bill. On the way to the car they all

agreed they needed to stop and spend some time visiting

Mark at the hospital.

Traffic was heavy and it took over 20 minutes to

get through crosstown traffic. They finally arrived at St.

Joseph's Hospital where Linda was slouching

uncomfortably in one of the waiting room chairs. It was

easy to see by her unkempt appearance that the long

night she had spent awaiting updates on Mark hadn't

allowed her much time for rest. The remnants of her

continental breakfast were in evidence on the small table.

Though she smiled and hugged each of them upon arrival,

her blood shot eyes told the truth. Mace asked her how

long it had been since she had slept, and she couldn't

even remember if she had gotten any sleep last night at all.

The doctor had come out around 2 a.m. and told her that Mark was a very lucky man. Had his stab wound been several inches to the left or had the weapon been an inch longer, he would have died of internal hemorrhaging. As it stood now, his renal artery had been slightly nicked by the puncture and required six stitches to close off the bleeding.

Mark had been in recovery for almost seven hours now and was due to be moved to his room sometime close to 10 o'clock this morning baring anything out of the ordinary. Linda had insisted on a private room paid for by the Safe House and had told the hospital staff to spare no expenses when it came to his level of care.

Glen had slipped off to the cafeteria while Linda and Mace were talking and was just now returning with a bacon, egg and cheese biscuit, which he handed to Linda. She graciously accepted his gift and proceeded to devour it in no time flat. Mace filled her in on the apparent monogram they had discovered on the rag and requested that they be allowed to use her computer and technical staff. She finished eating and grabbed her phone to call Jacob, the head of her computer support group. She told him what they needed and then handed the keys to the Safe House to Mace. Her eyes stared intently into his as she pleaded for him to go find whoever was responsible for the attacks. Mace kissed her softly and suggested that she go home and rest. She waved him off, and then the team turned and walked out of the sliding doors back to the car on the second floor of the parking garage.

Once seated and belted, they steeled their resolve regarding this case and bringing the perpetrators to justice. Donald Roy and Glen were to meet with Jacob and begin the process of sifting through the database searching for names that either began or ended with the letter "D". They would include either first name or last name. Karla and Mace planned to re-examine the hidden door area and the surveillance tapes further for additional clues. They arrived at the Safe House as the town square clock signaled 10:11.

Jacob was waiting by his black 1970 Challenger flipping a coin into the air and then snatching it with his right hand before flipping it again. His classic muscle car was black with chrome rims, a hood scoop and a white racing stripe around the rear of the vehicle. A spoiler, dual exhaust pipes and fender vents completed the modified look. Apparently not only was Jacob an excellent engineer in the computer field, he was also an aficionado of classic and antique automobiles.

Mace handed the key ring over to Karla and suggested they head inside to get started on this maze of information as soon as possible. She slipped the key into the lock, swung open the door, and stepped inside. Glen, Jacob, Donald Roy, and Mace followed her in and headed upstairs towards the offices feeling pretty good about their chances of finding the owner of the rag. Jacob coded the security number into the electronic lock before Mace joined Karla in the video room. Karla dropped her purse onto the table and she and Mace decided to retrace the steps the team had taken the night of the attack. Mace followed closely behind her jotting notes onto a pad from time to time as she recalled the events of that evening.

Karla sat and closed her eyes while trying to concentrate on the timeline desperately attempting to recall her experience. One new fact that came to light was that Karla had encountered one of the waitresses and the young woman wasn't wearing her nametag.

"Do you remember anything that stood out like a tattoo or scar or possibly a lisp?" Mace asked.

Karla again closed her eyes and tried to relive the encounter in her mind searching desperately for an answer to that question. Soon she smiled and said the woman had a rose tattoo on her ankle. Karla had seen it when she bent down to pick up the pen that had fallen from her hand when they bumped into each other. "Now we're getting somewhere," Mace said. "Keep trying, Karla. You can do it just take your time."

"Hey, Jacob, since this is your area of expertise, what do we do now?" Glen asked. Jacob replied, "I'm going to write a query using the letter "D" as my filter." Noticing the quizzical look on Glen's face, Jacob explained, "A query opens two windows on the computer screen. In the top window you type the question you are asking the program and hit the execute button. Through the inner workings of the software after a period of time, the results are displayed in the bottom window. The length of time it takes to show the results depends on how much data must be filtered through along with the complexity of the question being asked."

Jacob wrote the query into computer syntax and lowered his finger in a grand gesture down onto the execute key. He smiled smugly and sat back in his leather desk chair assuredly. Seconds later the screen began to blink and the timer began counting up from zero noting the elapsed time required to complete the search. Jacob told Glen and Donald Roy that although he had put the necessary parameters into the program, he was certain it would take a while before it could finish and present the results to them. He suggested that while they wait they should pass the time and humor him in a game of chess. Jacob displayed chess mastery and in only 5 moves he had Glen in checkmate. Glen remarked of Jacob's superior intellect and said okay wise guy, let's have a rematch. Once again

Jacob easily won in 7 moves. Donald Roy being much more more familiar with the game, caused Jacob to concentrate more intently on his strategy, but he eventually won by checkmate, also. Patience was not a virtue of Glen's when he was not involved in activities he enjoyed. He was becoming slightly agitated with Jacob and his condescending attitude, so he decided to join Mace and Karla downstairs.

Donald Roy and Jacob continued to test each other's skills for traps and pitfalls while discussing the intricacies of the case against him. It was now Jacob's turn to be awed by the bevy of evidence that seemed to point to the absolute guilt of Donald Roy for the twin murders of his wife and daughter. The tale of his ordeal told by Donald Roy had Jacob on the edge of his seat.

Jacob began to furrow his brow when he realized the enormity and complexity of the frame job. A look of bewilderment came over his face as Donald Roy laid out the time line and clandestine nature required to win Mace over to the believing of his innocence. He regaled Jacob with how Glen, Karla, and he had been trapped and questioned in the secret room before he was eventually knocked unconscious. Thankfully, Mace showed up and rescued the three of them while Mark was on his way to the emergency room. A long, slow gasp escaped the lips of Jacob, and he buried himself into the back of his chair almost in a state of shock.

"Wow!" he exclaimed. "Look, I'll help you guys in any way possible. If you need something else while you're here, I mean anything at all, just let me know."

Glen arrived with a sour look on his face as Karla was continuing her attempts to recall the details of the attack by closing her eyes as Mace prompted her with who, what, when, where, and how questions. As Karla spoke to Mace, Glen decided to join her in the exercise. This decision by Glen turned out to have a calming effect and helped ease his frustration towards Jacob and the chess match. Mace extracted every memory from the two of them, and they discovered that not only did this young lady in question have a rose tattoo on her ankle, but she was also wearing a ring on the third finger of her right hand also shaped like a rose. They next learned that it was between 9:45 and 10:10 at night because Glen had just looked at his watch and was counting down the time left until midnight. It seemed strange how the little details got lost and were seemingly forgotten, but being knocked unconscious had contributed to that.

They left the bar area where Mark had been standing and Karla helped recreate the crime scene with Mace posing as the victim and her as the criminal. Glen used his watch to time the events from start to finish. One minute and 18 seconds was all it would have taken for "D", which is what they had decided to call the unknown assailant, to walk across the floor, drop her pen, stab Mark in the back, and make her exit through the secret door. It appeared from the reconstruction that the stabbing was a clever distraction to keep Mace busy while she rendered Glen and Karla unconscious and questioned and warned Donald Roy. Now all they needed were the results from Jacob and the computer program.

Glen brought Mace up to speed on Jacob's attitude and penchant for the dramatic. He also suggested that if Jacob challenged him to a game of chess he should decline so as not to fuel Jacob's ego any further. Mace chuckled and said, "What makes you think he can beat me?" Glen shook his head in disgust and replied, "I can't be the only one of us who doesn't play chess great now. Can I?"

Karla quickly informed him not to include her in the group with him because she also relished the feeling she got when she conquered another chess player. "Fine," Glen grumbled as they walked up the stairs back to the computer room. "Okay, so I'm the only one on this team of brainiacs who doesn't play chess that well; I'm perfectly okay with that. I'm good at shooter games. So there."

"Calm down, big guy we're just yanking your chain," Mace said. A look of chagrin came over Glen's face and the three of them laughed the rest of the way down the hall. "I've got to admit it. You two got me good with that one. Just remember karma has a funny way of coming back to bite ya," Glen said. The laughter subsided

and Mace knocked on the door and waited for Donald

Roy or Jacob to open it.

The sound of footsteps was faintly audible before

the door swung open and Jacob invited them in to sit

down. They strode into the room single file as Donald

Roy was moving his white knight in an effort to put Jacob

in check. The move proved to be a mistake as Jacob took

the knight with his bishop and placed Donald Roy in check

instead. One more move was all that was required before

Jacob rung up another victory.

Now that Mace had his undivided attention, he

asked Jacob how long his query had been running. He

glanced over to the computer monitor and saw that the

script he had written had raised the timer to 45 minutes.

Mace asked, "How much longer do you think it might take

to complete?" Jacob answered, "Hard to tell, really. It

could be minutes or it could take hours, but one good thing is we have exclusive use of the computers until 5:30 when the workers arrive to clock into the system." Mace suggested they slip across the street for coffee while they waited. Even if the computer program was still running when they returned, he felt certain that they could all use the change of scenery.

As Mace walked into McDougal's Deli, memories flooded his mind of the first time he saw Linda and he smiled. He could almost picture her standing in that sexy black dress, wearing those red stiletto heels, her hair perfectly styled and looking absolutely stunning. The memory was so vivid, he could virtually feel the nervousness he'd experienced inside his stomach a couple of weeks back. He allowed himself the luxury of a few uninterrupted moments to relive that experience. Mace must've stopped walking or talking or listening because when he came back to reality everyone in the group was looking at him. Incredulously he asked, "Well, what are you all looking at? Haven't you ever seen a man in deep thought before?"

The four of them burst into laughter at Mace's expense and they found an empty table with five chairs, sat down and waited for a waitress. A few minutes passed before Naomi came over to the table and asked for their orders.

Karla, Jacob, Donald Roy, and Glen began to discuss the town and its attractions for visitors other than the Safe House. Mace decided to give Linda a call and see if Mark had made it to his room yet, since she was already on his mind.

After fishing the iPhone from his pocket, he found her name under favorite's numbers and tapped the screen to dial her cell. Shortly after their very first encounter when Mace almost couldn't find her number, he decided to add Linda to the list of his favorite contacts in his phone. Even as the phone was ringing he could faintly recall the scent of her perfume filling his nostrils. Memory lane was once again capturing his conscious thoughts as Linda's voice wafted into his ear, "Hello, Mace. How's it going over there? Is Jacob being helpful, or has he tricked you guys into playing chess with him? I forgot to tell you he played on his college chess team, and they won the national championship three years running. Watch out for him if he begins to try to get you to bet with him," she said laughing. "He's a master at tricking you into thinking you stand a chance for the first few moves, and then like a dagger to the heart he calls out checkmate. I'm sorry she apologized; I've been rambling here and don't even know what you called about. I guess the caffeine from that triple shot vanilla latte' is really working me over."

Her fast paced speaking didn't bother Mace in the least as he was enjoying listening to her voice. Mace asked her if Mark had made it to the room yet and she replied, "Yes, he has, and he's resting comfortably. I'm feeling much better knowing he's recovering so well too " she replied. Without realizing how bold he sounded, he told her, "We are going to find his attacker and you will be able to look them in the eye as the guilty verdict is announced, and that's a promise." Linda sighed and told him she had all the faith in the world in him and the team doing that very thing. She ended the call with a heartfelt request, "Go get them."

Mace hung up the phone, updated the team, and knew that the end was drawing near. Naomi returned with the food and drink so they had a moment of silence before toasting their cups to persistence. Now all that was left was for them to wait for those names.

The familiar ring tone Mace had set alerted him that a call was inbound from Joshua now. Mace allowed the song to play a few bars of the music before answering. "Hey, Mace," he heard the voice say, "This is Joshua. How's it going up there? Have you and the team uncovered any more evidence that could lead you to the real killer?" Mace waited for Joshua to take a breath before he replied, "Joshua, old buddy, I've been thinking of calling you with an update, but I've been rather busy. You see, one of Linda's best friends was stabbed and the team was attacked, but that just tells me that we're getting really close to solving this case now. The good news is everyone will be okay. Let Judge Winston know that I should have this case wrapped in a nice tidy bow for her by the end of next week."

"Seriously, Mace, in the next seven and a half days you'll know who killed Donald Roy's family?" Joshua asked. "You believe you're that close to catching the killer? Are you sure Donald Roy is innocent? You'll really be adding that old Mace the Ace Dugan legend if you can bring this case to a close that quickly".

Even as Mace promised Joshua that timeframe, the hairs on the back of his neck stood up on ends again. He figured that if he put a date out there, it would force him to make it happen. Plus, Mace knew that Joshua had to tell Judge Winston something. Not only was he seeking an update for himself, he also had to apprise his boss, the major partner of the law firm, Mr. Caston, of Mace's progress. Joshua sounded almost giddy as he told Mace that he could hardly wait to see the old man now and make his day with this fantastic news. "Bye,

Mace. I'll talk to you later," he said. Mace said, "Yeah,

man, I'll see you soon. Take care."

Chapter 5

Good News

Joshua headed straight to Judge Winston's office to bring her up to date on the progress Mace had made after he hung up the phone. He hardly noticed that traffic was bumper to bumper while he listened to the radio and made his way to the courthouse. Somewhat robotically his subconscious drove the car while he drummed on the steering wheel of his arctic white Mercedes Benz convertible to "I've Got the Power" by Snap and contemplated his probable partnership in the law firm. For seven long, hard years he had been employed at Caston, White, and Brockhoeft. Joshua had been hired as a clerk, before he had made associate in two short years and was believed to be on the fast track to becoming a junior partner. That accomplished, it would only be a matter of time before he was invited to become a full senior partner. His future had looked so bright until old man Caston had chosen Daniel to be the junior partner before him. Joshua never understood why Mr. Caston had promoted Daniel over him, but he continued to diligently practice the law to the best of his ability despite his resentment.

As Joshua strolled up the walkway leading to the courthouse steps, he had an irrepressible grin on his face. He knew that the moment he told Judge Winston that Mace had found Donald Roy, along with evidence that proved his innocence, the continuance he sought would certainly be granted. He was certain his prayers were going to be answered as he entered the judge's chambers. Joshua was surprised to learn that Judge Winston would have no part in allowing the continuance. In fact she wouldn't even agree to hear his motion stating that this alleged new information had no bearing on her ruling. Instead she stood firm upon her decision that Donald Roy surrender himself to Las Vegas authorities within the next four days or face additional charges. Joshua's confident grin quickly vanished upon hearing Judge Winston's sobering words.

The phone would be ringing in Mace's pocket making him aware of the day's proceedings once Joshua had left the courthouse. So there it was; Mace had to put Donald Roy on a plane in 72 hours to insure his arrival in Las Vegas met with Judge Winston's requirements or things could worsen. In fact, Mace, himself, could be charged with aiding and abetting a fugitive.

Mace and Jacob had just finished the snacks when Jacob suggested they get back over to The Safe House. Mace hadn't finished drinking his latte', so he asked Naomi for a "go cup". She took his cup with its remaining liquid and went to the counter to alert the barista that Mace would be taking his coffee to go. She had such a pleasant demeanor about her that Mace felt compelled to leave her a nice tip, so he put a five-dollar bill on the table.

The rest of the crew had already slipped on their coats and were heading to the front door for the dash across the street when Naomi came back and handed him a freshly made, full-sized latte'. She winked, smiled, and said, "Anytime you need a refill, just come look me up, Mace." His name lingered on her tongue, and she said she had overheard the others call him Mace. "I get off work at six. Perhaps we could go catch a movie," she said. "Naomi, I'm flattered, but I'm currently seeing someone," Mace replied.

"Just my luck," she said, "I finally find a hot guy to help warm my bed on these frosty winter nights, and he's already taken. Well, if things don't work out, you know where to find me."

He assured Naomi he would do just that as he thanked her for her interest and great service before hurrying to catch up with the team. Mace raised the collar of the leather jacket, slipped on his gloves, wrapped the muffler around his face and stepped out onto the sidewalk. The brisk north wind howled at him. He saw a break in traffic and scurried across the street to join the team. The snow was falling heavily again, and it blocked out any hint of the sun or its warmth. Jacob rapidly unlocked the door, and they all went inside to check on the progress of the query.

Sometimes in the wee hours of the morning, Mace would find himself contemplating how it was almost always the tiny details that cracked cases. Such was the instance around two this morning. Mace wondered if the deadline he had set and given to Joshua was attainable. Though it was still early in the race to the finish line, that being court in Las Vegas where Donald Roy would be exonerated, Mace couldn't help but feel some nervousness. Mace decided to remain downstairs to meditate on the facts alone instead of returning to the computer room with the others. He knew if they found anything solid, he would be informed post haste.

Jacob was topping the stairs with the remainder of the team close behind when Mace got an eerie feeling of déjà vu. What made Mace so good at his job was his military training. This background experience made him very attentive to details. If someone lines up the evidence in its chronologic order and dissects it, there is usually one glaring spot in the time line that shows inconsistency. It is here, at this point, that one realizes that the facts as they appear are wrong or misleading. It was time he found that point in this case or Donald Roy's innocence would become a moot point.

Coffee in hand, Mace walked to the bar, sat at the nearest table and reviewed the facts. A tablet was on the bar, so he picked it up and began the task of transferring the scribbled notes scattered on various pages in the pocket notebook to the neat graph he had drawn on the paper. He started the timeline with Donald's admittance into the Army and concluded it with the date of his arrival in Milwaukee. Mace filled in the blank spaces between with dates of his return from active duty, the meeting of his wife, their wedding date, the birth of their daughter, the purchase of their house, the first day on his job and various other events of significance in his life. It was quite a daunting task and Mace hadn't realized the length of time he'd put into its completion until his phone rang.

When he picked it up to answer the call he saw it was three forty-five in the afternoon.

The voice on the other end put an immediate smile on his face when she asked if he'd been missing her. "Yes, Linda, I have, and have you been missing me, too?" he asked.

"Oh, Mace, you know I have."

"How is Mark doing now?" Mace inquired. "Do you have anything new from the doctors?" "He's resting comfortably, extremely weak and tired, but he's already flirting with the nurses here. Reminds me of someone else...hmmm," she teased. "Was Jacob able to get any useable information for you?"

Mace told her that was indeed great news and that he would continue to pray for Mark. He told Linda he was downstairs working on a separate project while the others were all upstairs watching the computer and awaiting its results. She asked what he was working on, and Mace told her about the timeline and how he'd used it to solve numerous cases.

She said it seemed like a great idea to her and based on his past successes it was smart to take the time to construct it.

"How far have you gotten?" Linda asked.

"I was just applying the finishing touches when you rang," Mace said. "I'm glad you called for two reasons: I need to go check on the team and see where they stand and the sound of your voice always lifts my spirits and puts a smile on my face."

"Oh, Mace," she said, "you say the sweetest things a girl just loves to hear. Well, go check on the others before I start blubbering on this phone. Call me later. Okay?"

"I will, babe," he said. "Goodbye, babe."

"Goodbye, Mace".

Mace arose from the table with the trusty timeline in his hand and he walked over to the stairs. One by one he climbed the steps leading to the offices. As he did he mulled the reception he'd get from Donald Roy when he presented with the timeline project. Mace topped the stairs, arrived at the computer room door and knocked firmly. When it opened, he walked inside and sat down in the first available chair.

Glen asked where he'd been. Mace pointed to the timeline and Glen said, "Oh, it's that time again, eh? You know, Mace, I can't even count all of the cases you've broken open with that tool."

Donald Roy asked Mace what tool is it exactly that Glen was referring to.

Mace was about to launch into a long dissertation on the use of the drawing in his hands when the computer printer began to come to life.

"Eureka!" Jacob shouted. "We have completed the first phase of our research. Now that we have a smaller amount of data, we can continue to refine the criteria we are seeking, and it will be much faster, too".

"Okay," Mace said, "the first thing I want is to eliminate anyone deceased."

Jacob coded in some words and hit the execute button. Less than five minutes later, all of the deceased were removed.

"Now delete anyone who is less than five feet tall or older than fifty; there's no way those could have overpowered the team," Mace proposed. Three and a half minutes later, those were removed.

"Wow, you really know your stuff, Jacob," Mace said. "How many names are left in the list now?" he asked. Jacob replied that they were down to a couple hundred names left.

"Hmmm, still too many," Mace mused. "What else can we eliminate, I wonder? Let's eliminate anyone whose address is now overseas or who has an expired student or work visa."

"Oooh, good call, Mace," Jacob said.

"Since this is a college town we get a large number of students here on those. Just let me refine this query a little more," Jacob said.

His hands tapped on the keyboard and a long string of words and symbols appeared on the computer screen. Jacob typed and retyped the string several times before he was satisfied that this would eliminate the maximum number left in the results from the first run. He seemed quite pleased at his work when he leaned back in his chair as the computer once again began to make whirring sounds. Two minutes and seventeen seconds later he had narrowed the list from several hundred to twenty-six names. Jacob printed the list six times, one for each team member and a master copy.

"Now we've just got to burn through this list as quickly as possible," Mace said, "and we'll find our murderer/murderess."

Each team member went to a different office after being instructed to go to Google and find any information not listed on their sheets about the six names assigned them. Time was rapidly slipping away from them, and Donald Roy had less than sixty-six hours remaining before having to leave for Las Vegas.

Workers were arriving for their shifts and needing to clock into the automated time system. Jacob quickly started the programs he had shut down during his database search, the time clock software being one of them. Suddenly it dawned on him that they had fingerprint time clocks. The software had a digital image of each worker's fingerprint on his dominant hand. He clicked a few buttons, tapped a few more keys, pressed the left mouse button, and was surprised at what appeared on the screen.

Mace heard Jacob call his name, so he returned to the computer room where Jacob was grinning like a Cheshire cat. When Mace asked him what had him so happy, Jacob pointed to the screen and said, "Look what I just found while running a routine report of work schedule hours against actual hours worked. Her name is the only one to show up. Mace she was clocked in when Mark was stabbed and your team was attacked," Jacob said. Mace's jaw dropped as he read the name on the screen.

"Well, I'll be dammed," he said. "How do you suppose she managed to pull this off right under our noses? Furthermore, what could

possibly be her motive for attacking my team? Is

she working alone or in cahoots with someone?"

The time had come for an interrogation

to find these and answers to other questions that

were burning in his mind. Yes, he needed to have

a one on one discussion with Darla Landry, and

he'd have that discussion tonight if she showed

up for work.

According to the work schedule listings

she should be clocking in within the next thirty

minutes for her shift until close. Mace gathered

the team in Linda's office to apprise them of the

situation. Karla interjected that if Darla was

responsible for the attacks here, she had to have

an accomplice providing her with their comings

and goings. "We need to keep Darla from

becoming aware of our suspicions of her," Karla continued.

Glen suggested, "Maybe we could try to catch her after work."

"What if I invited her to go out with me after her shift ended?" Mace asked.

"Great idea," Glen interjected. "She would be away from the Safe House, her guard would be down, and we could capture her when you give the signal, Mace."

"When I'm walking the floor later, I'll accidentally bump into her and make the invitation," Mace said.

Jacob suggested that Mace invite her to Wicked Hop located just three minutes away at 345 N. Broadway. "Just take E. Wells to N.

Broadway and turn right. Go about a half a mile, and it's down on your right. Plus, they have great late night food, too, Mace," he said.

"I recommend that everyone stay sharp and focused tonight," instructed Mace. "Don't allow the ticking clock to cause any slip-ups. Whoever was working with Darla knew what they were doing and they seemed to be ready for us."

The team agreed and then began to fan out through the various rooms vowing to remain in constant contact and give Darla's position as soon as she was spotted. Jacob decided to stay in the computer room and monitor the time clock software for her clock in punch. Mace gave him a radio like the ones used by the team, and they performed a sound check.

"Glen, how do you read me?" Mace asked. The military term for good communication is 5 by 5, and this is was how Glen responded to the question. One by one Mace went down the roll call of team members over the radio with each replying the same as Glen. If this strategy played out the way he'd planned, in just a few hours they'd be interrogating Darla Landry and hopefully gathering intelligence that would help keep Donald Roy Perkins from going to prison.

Mace walked the floor and surveyed the room noticing couples who just didn't seem to belong together. "Love is blind," he mused. He was wondering how these couples might have met when the radio squawked.

"Mace, this is Karla. I don't see Darla anywhere around the restrooms."

"Okay, Karla. Keep sweeping the area back toward the bar then," Mace replied.

Jacob's voice came next saying, "She just clocked in so we know she's here." Mace told him to stay out of sight since he didn't normally walk the floors and to keep to the upstairs office area.

Donald Roy was the one who spotted her first. He excitedly blared into the radio and almost caused Mace to remove the earpiece so as not to cause permanent hearing loss. Calmly, Mace told him to lower his voice and call out her location. He said she was coming out of the employee dressing rooms and walking to the bar area where Jamie was supplying drinks to the wait staff. Mace spun around as Darla came walking through the main entrance. Mace watched her as she picked up an order pad and headed towards her assigned area. He decided to wait for a while before making the move so as not to spook her. Yes, this had to be played quite delicately, and he was just the man for the job.

When the time began inching its way towards eleven o'clock, Mace told the team who had kept Darla under surveillance all evening he was about to make the move and for them to watch his back. Each member signaled they were ready and Mace strolled over to the bar walking quite purposefully. About two thirds of the way there, he bumped into Darla and chatted with her for a few minutes. It seemed the thought of going out with Mace again was something she had been hoping for since they'd had so much fun last time even though they had both fallen asleep before having sex. As Mace recalled they had wound up spending the night together talking. The next morning they had lunch before he left for the airport to return home. Sometimes in the covert undercover world of detective/spy work, one can lose track of each target, so it's good to keep a journal. Mace enjoyed reviewing the notations he'd made before meeting with them again. This tactic allows for recall of certain things like locations, what they were wearing, what they did or ate, or any of their friend's names. This immediately puts the target at ease and the detective above suspicion.

Mace reminded Darla about their date and the Thai food they had for lunch the next day. She gave him that wicked grin and said since he hadn't called her she had assumed either he didn't enjoy their time together or had no real interest in seeing her. Mace reassured her that somehow they had gotten crossed signals, he told her tonight could be the beginning of fixing all that if she still wanted.

"Of course, I still want to, silly. These boys can't hold a candle to you, Mace," she purred. "I get off in an hour, and we can go back to my apartment again, if that's okay with you."

Mace asked her if they could get breakfast from the Wicked Hop first as he needed energy.

She giggled and agreed, "That would be a great idea."

Mace took one step toward the bar, turned his head back, and told her how glad he was that she had accepted his offer. "I'll see you in an hour right where we met last time, if it's okay with you, Darla."

"See you there, stud," she whispered.

Mace made his way past Jamie and into the back room that led to the cellar and storage area. It was much quieter back there, and Linda immediately came to his mind. It was tough on him deceiving Darla that way, and he wanted to tell Linda about the plan. Mace slipped his hand into his pocket, pulled out the iPhone and selected her cell number and was greeted by Linda's very sleepy sounding voice saying, "Hello, Mace, baby."

"Hello, doll, how are things going over there?" he inquired.

She said that Mark had eaten earlier, watched some television and then fallen back asleep. When the lights had been turned off in his room, she grabbed a blanket, curled up in the lounge chair, and drifted off to sleep dreaming about the life she knew the two of them could be living.

Mace apologized for waking her, but wanted to inform her of the plan tonight with Darla so she wouldn't hear it from someone else. With the recent events so fresh and the little scenario they had planned, he didn't want her to fear for his safety.

"Mace," she said, "I am glad you told me about your plan, and I trust your experience in situations like this. Do you really think it'll work?"

"It's got to," he replied. "Time is running short. I've got to do something drastic and unexpected."

"Please do whatever it takes to get the case solved short of killing someone, of course," she said as she laughed.

Mace told her to get some rest and he'd talk to her in the morning with an update regarding Darla.

"Good night, Linda," he whispered.

"Mmm, night, Mace," she replied.

The hour from eleven to twelve passed like seconds. While Mace waited outside for Darla, he began wondering once again about this case and its many twists and turns. If this trap worked as planned, soon he might finally begin to see the full picture instead of just one section of it. This case reminded him of an onion with its many layers. Each time one layer was peeled back, another would be revealed until the center exposed the heart of the issue. Mace was certain in his gut that Darla couldn't be in this mess alone and that if he squeezed her slightly, she would gush out the whole story to him.

The chilly night air produced a fog with each breath. His body shivered from the cold and the thoughts running through his mind. This had to work, and it was going to, he convinced himself. His instincts had gotten him this far in his career, and they would succeed again; he was certain of it.

Darla came out the door and waved for him to come and get in her Jaguar saying she'd drive them to Wicked Hop for breakfast. Mace strolled over, got inside the passenger seat, buckled the safety belt, and settled in for the short ride.

The streets were almost empty of traffic when Darla turned into the parking lot of Wicked Hop and parked right by the front door. She leaned over after turning off the ignition and asked if he was ready for the upcoming events of the night with her. Mace feigned his best smile and told her tonight would definitely be a night to remember.

Glen had parked the van facing backwards so the sliding door was on Darla's side. The instant she exited the car, he pulled a black knit bag down over her head and yanked her into the vehicle. Donald Roy then placed a similar bag over Mace's head and tossed him into the back with Darla. Glen drove the van and Karla got in the Jaguar to follow him.

The two vehicles proceeded to a hotel where an interrogation room had been set up earlier. Karla had stayed and watched Darla with Mace at the Safe House while Glen and Donald Roy slipped off to attend to this task. The capture had worked like a Swiss watch...perfectly.

When the bags were removed from their heads, Darla and Mace were in a small room, handcuffed together, and it was pitch black. Mace asked her if she was okay and she replied, "What the hell is going on, Mace?"

"I thought you knew, Darla, because I haven't got a clue."

"Aren't these people enemies of yours, Mace?"

"Not that I'm aware of. Are you involved in anything I should know about?" Mace asked.

With a panicked voice, he said if she had anything she needed him to know now was the opportune time to fill him in on the details before they came back and began questioning them.

She told him that she wasn't involved in anything and thought it might be because of his connection to the Donald Roy Perkins case.

The door swung open, and a very bright light shone on their faces. One of the masked assailants unlocked the handcuffs and grabbed Mace to his feet. A quick punch in the gut and then another to the face gave the appearance he was being roughed up with more to come. Mace told Darla to keep quiet and then he was hit on the back of the head and fell to the ground with trickles of blood at the corners of his mouth. Great little effect Karla had added by slipping the blood capsule in

Mace's mouth when Glen had jerked him to his feet
earlier.

Darla looked terrified, so they left Mace there and
took her into another room containing only a chair and a
high beam light shining directly down onto it. Darla was
seated, tied to the chair, and then the light was directed
into her eyes from a very close range. This technique
causes confusion and disorientation on the detainee
usually resulting in answers being given quickly unless the
one in question had special training on how to deal with
these situations.

Glen's navy seal training made him the perfect
person to interrogate Darla. He had a microphone
plugged into a voice synthesizer to disguise his voice. It
sounded as if it belonged in a horror movie. He spoke
very slowly so that his words hung in the air as he asked
repeatedly about her partner in the other room and what

they knew about Donald Roy Perkins. She tried to tell him they weren't partners but was told if she didn't start talking fast, they were going to be considered as loose ends that needed to be tied up, which meant both she and Mace were going to be killed if they didn't get the answers to their questions soon.

After realizing the futility of the situation, Darla cracked and said she had been hired by someone in Las Vegas to cause havoc and try to mislead Mace and his team. She told Glen that she received new instructions daily whenever Mace was in town but that she had nothing to do with the recent stabbing or attack on the team. She had been told that it was going to happen but had been so consumed with guilt that she went to the Safe House to warn Mark. It was already too late when she arrived. A woman dressed in all black told her to clock in and stay put or else she would meet with the same fate as Mark. She clocked in, stayed put as told, and then when she heard the siren of the ambulance she ran like hell to her car and drove off.

Glen asked Darla to explain her connection to Las Vegas or this mysterious woman who had hired her. She told him they had sent her pictures of her little sister leaving for school and in various locales throughout a normal day. If she refused to help, or if she went to the police, her sister would meet with harm. The woman told her she had connections with nefarious individuals who would enjoy the youthfulness of her sister before hooking her on drugs and using her as a prostitute. Afraid for her sister's safety she reluctantly agreed to their demands.

Glen then asked how they contacted her.

Darla replied saying that she would get a manila envelope under her door with a note telling her what to do and when. Soon she began finding envelopes containing thousands of dollars under her door from time to time with notes saying she had done a good job. While she wasn't happy being forced to help these people, she was using the money to pay back her student loans and save for law school.

"Do you have any of these envelopes still in your possession?" Glen asked.

"If I do, they are still in my apartment," said Darla. "I can take you there so you can see for yourself if you'd like. Just please don't hurt me."

"Okay, we'll talk to your partner, and then we'll make our decision," was her captor's response. Darla was led back to the room where Mace was being held. She was handcuffed to the chair once again, and then her head was covered with the black bag. Since she could no longer see what was happening, Glen and Mace fake fought for a few minutes before they led him to the other room for his "interrogation."

Once Mace was in the second room, Donald Roy, Glen, and Karla could hardly contain their enthusiasm. Karla quickly caught Mace up on what Darla had said, and they decided to see if they could get any evidence from the envelopes. The best plan would probably be to return Mace to Darla and have him convince her that they should cooperate by giving these people holding them whatever they wanted. After she was certain Mace was on her side, she and he would go to her apartment while Glen and the team followed closely behind in the van. Darla would give Mace the envelopes and anything else she had received from the unknown Las Vegas woman and he would walk it to the van. If they were satisfied, both Darla and he would be released and allowed to live.

It didn't take much convincing at this point for Darla to agree to the idea. So they were allowed to get into her car with Mace driving, of course, go to her apartment, and do as they'd been instructed.

Three manila envelopes, almost five thousand dollars in one hundred dollar bills, and a single note was all that was left of the prior transactions. Mace put all of this into a bag and slowly walked out to the van to deliver it to the "kidnappers" as Darla watched from the window.

The plan had worked to perfection. Glen grabbed the bag, shoved Mace away, and slid the van door closed. One domino had fallen, and now it was up to Karla and the team to find the next clue.

Glen, Karla, and Donald Roy sped away in the van as Mace walked back to Darla's apartment complex. She seemed nervous now that the ordeal was over. Mace asked her if she had any real feelings for him to which she wistfully replied, "No, Mace. I'm sorry. I was only trying to save my little sister. Can you ever forgive me?" He assured her that he held no hard feelings towards her and that if the shoe were on the other foot, he'd have done the same thing to her if necessary. She smiled and asked, "What do you want to do now?"

"Why don't you drive me back to the Safe House where my car is parked, and then we can go our separate ways," he said. Mace told her that should she receive any communications from Las Vegas he should be informed immediately. She eagerly agreed to do so. "You're really not a bad guy, you know," she told him.

"You're no leftover meatloaf yourself, Darla," Mace teased.

With that said they got into her car and drove the three or so miles back to 779 N. Front Street.

Mace watched Darla's car until she made the turn onto E. Clybourn Street, which feeds Interstate 794, before he finally let down his guard and breathed a deep sigh of relief. The Monaco Blue Metallic BMW M5 rental car driver's door unlocked when he pressed the key fob and he climbed inside, buckled in, and began driving to link up with the team. Since the last time Karla had used her evidence kit and come up mostly empty, he knew she'd be anxious to get started on those envelopes and the cash. If they had just the slightest amount of luck on their side, someone had left a fingerprint or some trace evidence leading to the identity of what he now dubbed the "Las Vegas connection."

As Mace was tooling along the road he drifted into a somewhat hypnotic state. It seemed as though he blinked once and that car had teleported the usual twenty minute drive to the hotel almost instantly as he found himself turning into the parking lot. He quickly saw an empty spot and pulled in eager to get inside and get an update.

The blood from the pellet Karla had slipped into his mouth earlier was still visible at the edge of his lip. When Mace walked into the room and the team turned to see him, they all broke out into laughter.

Glen said, "Hey, Mace. You can clean your face now; the game is over."

Mace shrugged his broad shoulders, walked into the bathroom, grabbed a washcloth and dabbed at the red mark until it was gone. "So tell me, you guys," he said. "How terrified was Darla? It didn't take old heartless Glen Stevens very long to crack that little acorn, now. Did it? It's good to see you haven't lost your touch, old buddy," Mace said.

Glen chuckled and said he hoped that pawn recovered from his tactics rapidly.

"What about her sister, Mace? How are we gonna stop that tragedy from happening?"

asked Glen. They vowed they'd solve this case and her little sister would be safe because whoever was behind this would all be rotting in prison soon instead of Donald Roy Perkins.

Karla was hard at work lifting fingerprints from the envelopes and testing them against the time clock file Jacob had copied and given to her. The first match was understandably Darla's thumbprint, presumably put there from counting the money once she received it. However, the second print came up empty, which Karla said was a great sign. This meant that it could belong to the" Las

Vegas connection."

"How will we find out, Karla?" Donald Roy asked.

"We'll leave here tomorrow, and when I get back

to my lab in Las Vegas with the proper tools, I'll find out

who's a match to it. That's how," Karla stated

emphatically.

Glen was elected to acquire the flights back to Las

Vegas. Mace went to the hospital to be with

Linda and Mark. Karla and Donald Roy, both

facing severe exhaustion, decided to try to get

some sleep before relieving Glen afterwards.

Glen picked up the phone as Mace headed out

the door.

The moon shone brightly, reminiscent of

a giant spotlight overhead. Off in the distance

Mace could hear the faint sound of a train whistle as the locomotive made its way out of town. The night was still except for a gentle wind blowing the lightly falling snow as it stretched to reach the ground from somewhere above. Mace paused to take in the calmness and realized for the first time in almost thirteen months now, he too had peacefulness inside. Was it the fact that another piece of the puzzle had fallen into place? Was it the knowledge that Mark would recover? Was it the discovery of why Darla had gotten involved in this case? Maybe it was that he knew he was heading home tomorrow, with the best group of friends a man could hope to gather. Whatever the reason, he was happy to be caught in that moment of time and he languished for a few minutes. Mace stuck out his tongue catching a few of the white flakes before smiling to himself and walking over to the rental car to depart the hotel for the hospital and to see Linda one last time.

Mace listened to Christmas carols on FM 95.7 as he enjoyed the holiday season's glad tidings. Would he find Mark and Linda both asleep at this early morning hour? The dashboard clock showed almost 2 a.m. He'd probably have to do some major flirting and schmoozing to even get past the reception desk and security guard. Perhaps he should wait until later in the morning before attempting to link up with Linda. Yes, it was definitely too late to see her and explain the events of the past evening, so he decided to just enjoy a short drive.

Mace drove down to the river, stopped at McKinley Park and Marina, got out and walked along the waterfront enjoying the way the moonlight seemed to dance on the lake. After walking for about ten minutes he turned and ambled back taking in the crispness and solitude of the evening. A fresh perspective now gained, he was prepared for the remainder of this race for justice. As he was standing in the cold night air he achieved a Zen-like realization that tomorrow, back in Las Vegas, the final lap would begin in what had been a thirteen month marathon. He left the lake front to sleep and recharge his batteries; something told him he was going to need every ounce of his ability to win this one.

Morning broke and the sunlight shone through the thin curtains found in most hotel rooms. Silence filled the room except for faint snoring from Glen. He was rolled up in his blanket and only his head stuck out. He looked as though he were wrapped in a cocoon. Karla was sprawled across her bed one leg out from under the covers exposing her Minnie Mouse pajama bottoms.

Donald Roy slept on his side curled in the fetal position and clutching his pillow with a vise like grip.

Mace rose from the bed and made the short trek to the bathroom, stubbing his toe on Donald Roy's already packed suitcase as he did. Still not quite awake, Mace barely uttered an "ouch," but knew he would feel it later in the day. He had no sooner finished zipping his jeans when the phone rang with the wakeup call startling everyone. Glen lifted the receiver, waited for the message, and then placed the phone back on its cradle. "What time do our flights depart for home?" Mace asked. "Well, I figured you'd want to tell Linda goodbye, Mace, so I booked Donald Roy, Karla and me, on an 11:40 morning flight and you on the 9:10 departure this evening," Glen replied.

"You understand me better than anyone else, Glen," Mace told him.

"Thanks, pal," he responded. "Need a ride to the airport, or have you got that covered, too?" Mace asked.

"Taxi will be here to collect us about 9:30. We've got this covered. You go check on Linda, and I'll see you back in Las Vegas," Glen said.

"Done," Mace said. "Be careful, all of you. Okay? I'll see you this evening after I land. Drinks on me," he promised.

"Later, Mace," Karla stated as Mace headed out the door.

Linda was sipping coffee and Mark was still asleep when Mace arrived at the hospital room door. Though he tried to hide the inner conflict, Linda saw right through him. "What's wrong, Mace? You look troubled this morning," she said. He suggested they walk down to the cafeteria, find a table affording some privacy, and he'd fill her in on the case. She rose to her feet, and they hugged momentarily. Then she gave him a soft, short kiss and said, "Okay, babe. Let's go, then."

The cashier rang the total for Mace's two eggs, sausage, hash browns, two large coffees and Linda's muffin. She recommended a table in the corner, and they sat down in the brown, plastic chairs. Mace sprinkled some salt and pepper on the eggs, added creamer and three Splenda packets to his coffee, cut a big bite and raised the fork to his lips. As a man of action more than words, he searched his mind for the proper phrases to tell Linda how he felt about her while updating her on the latest news regarding her employee. Her crystal blue eyes were looking directly into his hanging on each word as he droned on about the case.

Finally, he had to tell her that he was booked on the 9:10 flight back to Las Vegas and wasn't sure how long he'd be gone this time. A bit startled, she replied, "But, Mace, that doesn't give us much time, and I have so much to say to you." He invited her to have lunch with him before he had to leave for the airport and she accepted. They decided that would be the best chance to say their goodbyes.

Mace grabbed his iPhone and searched the contact list for Bonnie's cell number. Selecting it, he pressed the call now button on the touch screen and awaited her voice on the other end. "Hey, Bonnie, it's Mace. I'm sending the team home to Las Vegas today on the 11:40 morning flight, and I need you to make arrangements for Donald Roy and Glen to stay somewhere safe and quiet. Meet them at the airport, and give Glen the details of the location you found. I'll be coming back tonight on the 9:10 flight, and I'll get my car from long-term parking. I'll call you when I arrive, and you can fill me in on any progress made. This case is starting to crack, Bonnie, and I'm about to find out who has been behind this frame job and the attacks on the team. I've gotta run right now, but let me know if you have any difficulty with my request. Bye, Bonnie."

"Bye, Boss."

After hanging up the phone, Mace decided now was a great time for him to get back to the hotel and pack. Hopefully stuffing clothes, shoes and various other items into the suitcases would not only take his mind off the case for a little while, but would allow him to formulate the words he wanted to tell Linda. Mace remembered her telling him that she thought they made a great couple and that she would love to continue the journey of getting to know each other more deeply. Though she and Mace were on opposite ends of the spectrum socially, he couldn't help but wonder what a life with her would be like. Could he be happy being true to one woman? Would he enjoy the comfort of knowing they would always be there for each other? How would he fit in with her friends who are all wealthy? Was he fit for the dinner party and charity ball lifestyle or was he a little too rough around the edges? Had he actually fallen in love with her or was he simply infatuated with the thought of being in love? Mace waved his hands around his head as to shoo those thoughts from his mind then finished loading his luggage.

He glanced down at the phone for the time, and noticed that checkout time wasn't that far off. He made his way to the front desk, rang the service bell, waited for Margaret the hotel desk clerk, to appear and told her he was ready to check out.

She asked the room number and Mace replied, "It's 426." Margaret clicked a few times with her mouse and then asked, "Are you Mace Dugan?"

"That's me, darlin'," he said.

"Alright, Mr. Dugan. Would you like us to bill the card we have on file for you?"

"Sure thing," he replied. "That would be perfect."

"Yes, sir. I'll need to have you sign the itemized billing sheet and then you'll be on your way. Did you enjoy your stay with us?" she asked.

"Why, yes I did," he told her and added that the hotel restaurant had a breakfast service that was out of this world.

She giggled and said she too enjoyed that service every chance she got. The printer ejected the bill, she placed it on the counter, handed Mace a pen and he

signed on the dotted signature line. Mace assured her

that if he ever needed to return to Milwaukee, he would

indeed being staying in their hotel once again. Of course,

in the back of his mind, he knew if things worked out

between him and Linda, there wouldn't be a need for a

hotel room next time.

Mace loaded the trunk with the suitcases and

closed the lid. The sun was shining through the clouds of

a beautiful ice blue sky. It belied the fact that it was

barely twenty-one degrees outside as the brightness

caused him to put on sunglasses to protect against the

glare. Linda and Mace had agreed that he would pick her

up at the front door at noon and they'd go to Sala Da

Pranzo Italian Restaurant for lunch. When he arrived at

11:57, she was already outside waiting for him. Mace put

the BMW in park and got out to open Linda's door. She

slipped into the heated seat and buckled in as he scurried

back to the driver's side. Mace leaned over, kissed her,

and slid his hand up her neck to pull her closer as he did.

Her perfume lingered in the air, and he commented on

how wonderful she smelled. After buckling his safety belt

and putting the car in drive, he typed the address of the

restaurant into the GPS and pulled away from the curb.

His heart began to race as he contemplated lunch with

this beautiful lady and wondered what she wanted to tell

him.

They arrived at the restaurant near the college

campus after the twenty-five minute drive over. Linda

informed him that this was one of her favorite restaurants

in the Milwaukee area, and it had been too long since she

had eaten there. Sala Da Pranzo is Italian for "the dining

room." This wonderful eatery was quiet with a cozy feel

and ambiance of Italy in springtime. They were escorted

to a booth and told the server would be with them shortly. Linda slipped into one side and Mace onto the bench opposite her. Each perused the menu separately, and she decided on the Noce salad while Mace chose the Chicken Parmesan and a cup of Minestrone soup. Each had selected an Italian cream soda to accompany the meal. Marcus, a young college student, was the server who took their order and then returned with warm bread and olive oil plus a small cup of marinara sauce for dipping.

Mace was more nervous than he had thought he'd be, and the conversation between them was strained for the first time. Neither of them was prepared for the talk they'd planned, so instead they sat and ate in mostly silence. As the tension rose it became unbearable for Mace, and Linda finally spoke first saying, "Mace, I understand you've got to finish this case, but I wanted you to know that I have developed deep feelings for you. I've become so fond of you and our time together that I find myself daydreaming of a life with you. We could travel, so you wouldn't get bored, or move to a warmer climate. I'd be willing to entertain any ideas you have if you feel the same way about me. Mace, I think I love you."

There were those three little words that could bring a man to his knees that could cause him to rethink everything about being a bachelor and living the carefree lifestyle. This fantastically beautiful, sweet, wonderful woman was offering Mace her heart and a life of leisure and travel if he desired it with her. Unfortunately, his old habits kicked in and he told her that her offer was very tempting, but that right now he could only concentrate on solving this case.

"After this case is closed, maybe we could discuss it further," he stammered.

The smile disappeared from her face and she suggested that he drive her back to St. James Hospital. Mace gulped down the remainder of the cream soda, threw forty-five dollars on the table, and grabbed his leather jacket. He unlocked the doors with the car fob, but Linda got in before he could open her door. As she sobbed silently on the trip back, Mace tried to explain his thoughts all the while feeling torn. The car pulled up to the curb and she finally turned and looked him in the eyes. She told him to have a safe flight home and to think about her offer. Instead of coming to the airport and seeing him off though, she decided to stay with Mark. Linda felt that watching Mace leave amid the emotional turmoil was more than she could handle right now. She disappeared inside the hospital, and he took off for the airport.

Maybe he could get the flight moved up or maybe he'd enjoy the lounge before departing for home. Either way, it was time to change his focus back to the case. Besides, there would be plenty of time to consider all of the possibilities of a life with Linda later. Mace knew that he needed to refocus his thoughts and complete the job he was contracted to do.

Chapter Six

A Bag of Snakes

The desk at the Avis rental car return had about six people ahead of Mace. This served as a nice pause in his day after the whole failed conversation with Linda. The lady in front of him made polite conversation about how insufferable waiting in lines could be unless she talked to someone to pass the time. She informed him that her name was Sunshine, but her friends call her Sunny. She wore a light blue business suit, which complemented her black hair nicely. Mace sized her up in a minute. Her makeup was clean and professional yet it highlighted her facial structure well. She stood tall and had perfect posture. Mace surmised she had a good education as spoke with perfect diction. Perhaps she would be a great distraction while he waited to see if he could be bumped to an earlier flight.

"Hi, Sunny. I'm Mace," he replied.

She said she was headed down to Las Vegas for a job interview with a property management company. The name of the firm was Terra West, and they had found her resume through a job placement service. Mace told her that he was on the 9:10 to Las Vegas himself but arrived early so he could enjoy the lounge area. Sunny said she was on a different flight but would love to chat some more in the lounge if Mace didn't mind.

"I don't mind at all, Sunny, "was Mace's reply. It was at this moment that Thomas, the clerk, motioned that she was next and he could help her. Another clerk came out and took Mace's keys, inspected the car, and closed the ticket. Mace grabbed the handle of the pull cart, picked up his duffel bag, and headed through the sliding doors towards the lounge with Sunny right behind him.

Because Mace is a frequent flyer he was able to use the special president's club lounge area. He carried a card in his wallet, which he presented to the electronic lock and gained entrance as the door released. In these exclusive lounges, one's luggage could be checked while the traveler enjoyed free drinks. A television, comfortable recliner chairs, tables, and wireless Internet were also available for one's comfort.

Sunny and Mace made their way to the bar where he ordered a Michelob with a Makers Mark chaser and she said, "I'd like to try the same thing." They chose a table after getting their drinks and sat down to enjoy them. The friendly staff inside came over and asked if they'd like to express check their bags or if any assistance was needed with their flights. The idea of express check sounded great to Mace, and he agreed that he would indeed like to avail himself of this service. Meanwhile he later discovered Sunny had her flight changed to match his. As he drank the beer and slammed back the first shot of whiskey, the stress of the day slowly began to escape his body. He immediately ordered a second round as Sunny followed his lead and drained her shot glass, as well. The hours passed like minutes as they drank and watched Sports Center on the plasma television set while making idle chit chat. Sunny asked Mace about fun things to do and see while she's in Las Vegas. Mace made several recommendations of what she should see and what to avoid at all costs. Soon the airline agent announced the 9:10 Midwest Airlines flight to Las Vegas, Nevada, would be boarding in ten minutes at gate D49.

First class passengers were always allowed to board before everyone else, so Sunny and Mace walked up to the gate agent and were ushered right aboard the jet. Whether it was the long day or the alcohol he'd consumed, once seated Mace immediately began to feel drowsy and soon drifted off to sleep. When he awoke, the flight attendant informed him they were still two hours out of Las Vegas. Mace looked around and found that Sunny was still asleep.

What a dream he had just had! He saw Donald Roy Perkins walking out of the Las Vegas courthouse with a huge throng of reporters all asking him if he felt vindicated now that he had been proven innocent. He was about to reveal who had actually murdered his family when the dream ended abruptly waking Mace. His conversation with the flight attendant roused Sunny. Peering through the dim lighting, she asked Mace what was going on. He explained what he did for a living and filled her in on some of his skip tracer/bounty hunter career. They talked for the remainder of the flight home and she tried to decipher the meaning of the dream. Without Glen present he was happy to have someone act as a sounding board and Sunny was more than willing to be this for Mace. With time trudging ever forward, he really had to double the efforts and leave no stone unturned. Home, that's where he'd find the final few clues to close this, case and it was getting ever closer with each passing mile.

The pilot spoke over the intercom that they would soon be landing and that it was time for the flight attendants to ready the cabin. This meant it was time to gather all cups and plates from the passengers. The tray table would need to be returned to its full and locked position along with the seat backs. One final pass down the aisle and they were set. The flight attendants alerted the captain and then buckled themselves in as well. The wheels made that familiar screeching sound as they came into contact with the asphalt runway.

Questions that needed answering flooded into Mace's mind. Had Karla made any progress as to the identity of the fingerprint she had discovered on the money? Were Glen and Donald Roy tucked away somewhere quiet and safe as he had instructed Bonnie? What could Donald Roy have done in his past that caused this to happen? Had Mace somehow missed something on his timeline?   Did his wife have someone with a grudge against her that put him in this situation? Would he discover that this was merely a random act of violence? Answering these questions would surely burst this case wide open.

Mace passed through the doorway of the plane, down the jet way, passed the ticket agent, and headed straight for the baggage claim area. Sunny caught up to him at the luggage turnstile stand. The first person Mace called was Karla to see if she had made any progress with the unknown fingerprint found on the money. Her voice was a little strained as she explained she had only been home for a short period of time and was hard at work searching different databases for a match. Mace hung up with Karla and dialed Glen. He said they had found the house Bonnie told him about, and it was hidden in some trees on the outskirts of town. He'd set up watches for the night with Donald Roy knowing that the time to turn him in to Judge Winston was right around the corner. As a team, they had less than 48 hours to wrap up this case. The last person Mace called was Joshua. He alerted him that they were all back in town and very close to figuring

out this mystery.

Mace reached out and plucked his luggage from

the moving belt. Then he turned and helped Sunny

gather hers, as well. She thanked him and wished him

success with the case and he wished her success with her

job interview then they bid each other goodbye. Meeting

Sunny reminded him that although he thought he knew

his friends, sometimes they would have secrets they'd

prefer never be found. This got Mace's mind racing in a

new direction, and he headed straight over to talk to Glen

and Donald Roy after loading the trunk and paying the

parking fee. One of the case buster questions needed

answering, so he pushed the accelerator a little bit harder

towards the floorboard and the car responded with a roar

of the engine.

The warm breeze and star-filled night sky made the ride over to the see Glen and Donald Roy a pleasure. Mace's body tingled as he was engulfed by the sensations of the climate changes. Mace turned the car into the driveway, followed it up to the house, and parked beneath the nearest tree. His headlights reflected off the chrome mufflers of Glen's Harley Davidson. He must have picked it up after Bonnie dropped them off from the airport. Glen always loved riding his Harley every chance he got.   Glen chose the midnight black metal flake powder coated engine against all that chrome to make it truly stand out in a crowd. His 6', 245 pound, ex-linebacker body fit that motorcycle like a glove. Mace shut off the engine before swinging open the door and quickly making his way to the stoop and knocking. Glen answered and Mace walked inside to the bar and sat down as they handed him a cold Michelob Ultra. Donald

Roy was just dressing after his shower, and Mace told him to sit down because he had some questions that he needed to ask him. Donald Roy plopped onto the bar stool next to Mace and Glen handed him a beer, as well. Mace explained that on the return trip home, a new idea had crossed his mind. "Remember when we first met, Donald?" Mace asked. "We tried to write down every name and possible motive an enemy could use against you. Is it possible you may have overlooked anyone? Tell me about your life before marriage; and try to be as detailed as you can." Glen passed a pen and pad to Mace, turned off the television, grabbed himself a fresh beer, and then sat down to assist with note taking of his own.

Donald began with his Ranger training and enlistment into the military. "Could anyone from your old team have it out for you from a mission gone badly?" Mace asked. Donald replied that all of the missions he had executed with his team had been rousing successes. He was still friendly with the two men that had survived their final foray twelve years ago and refused to accept the possibility, however minute, that one Army Ranger would turn on another.

"Okay, okay," Mace said, "then what was your life like prior to your service?" Donald replied that he was a college student at the University of Florida for five years before his entrance into the military. The Fighting Gator Battalion class had caused him to want to serve his country after college graduation. He had met a girl named Rhonda Russell during his freshmen year and thought that she would be his future wife. After two years together, their relationship had gone awry because he had to work to pay his tuition; plus he was often gone on various training camps with the army. Missing too many weekends and holidays along with the requirements for six weeks of summer tactical training proved to be more than Rhonda was willing to endure. The wedding had been cancelled, and he poured himself into his schoolwork.

"Have you seen or heard from her since then, Donald?" Mace asked.

"No, Mace, after our breakup she left school and moved away to live with her mom."

"Were there any fellow classmates that felt you got promoted or treated better than they did who would want to give you some payback?" Mace asked.

"Since I was a sophomore, I've dedicated myself to being the best of the best, Mace. That's why I chose the Rangers. I sculpted my body with countless hours of exercise and weightlifting. After waking every morning at five o'clock, I'd run for miles to increase my endurance. I even made friends with the custodian of the swimming pool, so I could practice my water treading skills and swimming abilities. If any of my classmates thought I got preferential treatment, they were dead wrong," Donald Roy said emphatically. "I earned everything I've gotten, and my only regret is that it has cost the lives of my wife and daughter," Donald said. "You've got to help me learn why this happened to me, Mace. You've just got to."

"We're close, Donald Roy," Mace said, "really close." He was just about to ask Donald another question when the IPhone buzzed signaling a call. "Damn!" Mace said. "We've been at this for a little over two hours, now. Let's take a little break while I take this call, guys. Besides, my stomach is telling me it must be getting close to breakfast time."

Karla's voice bellowed in the receiver, "Mace, I've found out whose fingerprints were on the money! You're not going to believe the name that showed up as the match. I was completely shocked. I've got to tell you," she continued.

"Okay, Karla, who is it?" Mace asked. Karla indicated that it might be safer considering everything that had happened to the team and all for him to come to her lab and see for himself. She was right, and Mace told her so before he hung up the phone. Glen had overheard just enough of the conversation to cause him to ask, "Hey, Mace, what was that all about?"

" Glen, old boy; you, me, and Donald Roy need to get over to Karla's lab immediately," Mace said. "The fingerprint match on the money has been made, and we need to gather the team to plan our next move." With that said, the three of them got up and went outside. Donald Roy and Glen slipped on their helmets as the big bike's engine roared to life. Mace buckled in and they drove off headed to the lab hurriedly because they now

had less than thirty hours to solve the case.

Though it was early morning with the sunlight

beginning to spill over the city, a cool breeze blew and the

temperature was in the mid-sixties. Mace decided to

leave the top up on the Saturn Sky. Forgoing the early

morning radio zoo shows, he chose the quiet as his mind

worked feverishly to guess the name of the culprit who

had left the fingerprint. He saw the familiar porch light

glowing, illuminating the door as he steered the car next

to Karla's in the carport. The gravel crunched under the

tires and the brakes made a slight squeal as they came to

a stop. Glen's rumbling "hog" pulled in right behind

Mace, idling to a rest before he shut off the engine. Karla

swung open her front door and excitedly gestured for

them to come inside. Mace threw the car in park,

grabbed the keys, pushed open the car door and followed

her, Donald, and Glen through the entrance. She had left the name on the computer screen and Mace felt his knees buckle beneath him as he read the name Maggie Ann Winston.

"Why would her fingerprints be on the money if she weren't involved?" Mace queried. He pondered calling the police, but with only circumstantial evidence he knew the case wouldn't stick. How was he going to interrogate her to get to the bottom of this if he didn't have enough evidence to have her arrested? Perhaps he could invite her out to eat and tell her a tale of murder, mystery, and mayhem that included known facts and see if she would let something slip. Meanwhile, Glen, Donald Roy, and Karla would have to search the records of Margaret Ann Winston to find the missing link that would finally put the proper perspective on this case. Maggie had been a friend of Mace's for several years, so he felt certain she would join him for supper tonight at Franco's, her favorite restaurant.

The private line rang in Maggie's home. She lifted the receiver to her ear and said, "Hello."

"Hi, Mags. It's Mace. I know you're really busy right now, but could the two of us meet for supper tonight around eight o'clock? I just got back in town late last night, and I think we should discuss how you want me to bring Donald Roy Perkins to your courtroom. Plus, since I've been gone for over a year, I could use some great Italian food and a bottle of that wine you've been raving about for so long. What do you say?" Mace asked. She delayed answering for a few seconds before agreeing that it sounded like a nice idea. She suggested that they meet there since he wasn't only her friend but a skip tracer who was under orders to deliver an escaped person back to her courtroom. She didn't want any appearances of impropriety or a lack of professionalism. "Too many tongues wag in this town," she said and she had her reputation to uphold.

"Sure. That'll be perfect because I've got a few errands to run between now and then anyway. See you there," Mace said. "Bye, Mags."

"Bye, Mace," she replied.

It was decided that the four of them would report to the library, use the Internet, and 35mm film readers to search through old newspapers for some catastrophic event that must have occurred in Maggie Winston's past. Once that was established, they would ferret out the connection to Donald Roy Perkins providing them with the reason that his wife and daughter had been killed. They hit the front door of the library just as it was opening for the day. The first stop was the public computer section where each sat down and began to search the Internet starting with Google.com. Thousands of results were returned for the name Margaret Ann Winston. They decided to try her college records next, but couldn't recall where she had attended. A quick phone call to Joshua brought about the answer. He said she had gone to college at the University of Chicago and proudly displayed her law degree on the wall behind her desk in her office. When Mace told the team of this news, it was as if another piece of the puzzle had just been revealed.

Glen was the first of them to get a hit on the Chicago Sun-Times. He found a small article regarding the law student's mock trial exercise of a case revolving around a double murder. Further digging through the story mentioned the name of the prosecutor, Clay Feinstein, the public defender was Tony Dickerson, and the judge was none other than Margaret Winston.

Maggie's roommate and sorority sister Rebecca Martin

portrayed the defendant, who according to the police

report, had killed her husband and son, yet maintained

that she was innocent. The exercise was based on an

actual case from years before that had ended with a hung

jury due to the lack of forensic evidence since DNA testing

didn't exist at that time. The similarities between the two

cases were too strong to dismiss wholesale. Glen decided

to handle the phone call to the college to see if he could

garner any additional details while the rest of them hit

the film readers. Karla took the obituaries and Donald

Roy the front- page section of the newspapers. Mace was

given the rest of the paper and the team began to delve

into the past. Time moved like a log on a raging river

making its way downstream to the waterfall. When Mace

gave his weary eyes a rest from staring at the small

screen, he checked his watch. Five hours had been spent

reading and searching, but so far he had found nothing.

Mace checked with the others and they reported the

same results. Since the amount of time before he had to

meet Maggie was quickly dwindling, he left the three of

them and hailed a taxi back to his place. The fare for the

cab ride home came to nearly twenty-five bucks. Mace

tossed in an extra five for the tip and dashed up to the

front door.

A cold beer, followed by a long nap, helped ease

some of the tension. All had been quiet since his arriving

home, and he decided a hot shower was just the medicine

needed before dressing to meet Maggie. Something in

his psychological makeup whenever he was around water,

be it hot tubs, beaches, or in any other form, always

helped invigorate his body and keep him focused on the

task at hand. Today was no exception to that rule. As he

lathered his arms, he reflected on the evidence and allowed his mind to play out different conclusions regarding this case. How could he approach Maggie without tipping his hand to the fact that all indications pointed to her involvement? It would take every ounce of tact and deftness he could muster to probe this point and still keep their friendship intact.

Franco's was only a few miles away from his condo, so he decided to leave around 7:30 since they had reservations. The restaurant was a swanky four-star eatery that required men's attire to be suit and tie to gain entrance. Mace had decided tonight, however, to wear a classic Ralph Lauren, three button, black tuxedo usually reserved for weddings and award banquets. The maître d' knew that Maggie was a judge, and Mace needed to look the part of a business acquaintance meeting her there. Platinum, monogrammed cuff links, the Cartier

Santos 100XL timepiece, and some black Ralph Lauren Andando Oxfords completed his outfit. Though he would never pay eight thousand dollars for a watch, whenever Mace wore it, he fondly recalled winning it on the greatest gambling night of his life playing Blackjack. Perhaps that's a story best left for another time...

Before he headed out the door to his car, Mace gave a quick call to Joshua to bring him up to speed on the latest developments in the case. After he answered the phone with his usual flair, Mace told Joshua he was meeting Maggie for supper tonight and would be turning Donald Roy over to her tomorrow morning at ten o'clock in her courtroom as per her orders. He practically squealed with delight and said, "You know, Mace, everyone was right about you being the best! Man, am I ever glad that you caught that guy and saved my job in the process. You have been an integral part of what will soon be my partnership in the law firm, and I'm not going to forget you either. When this is over, I want to take your entire team out for drinks and a nice meal on me. How does that sound?" Joshua asked.

"I'm sure that we'd all be excited to have a party on your dime, buddy," Mace replied chuckling aloud.

The thought of dining out at her favorite restaurant with a ruggedly handsome escort afforded Maggie the perfect opportunity to indulge in another of her passions that being high fashion. She skimmed through her closet and found her most prized ensemble consisting of a black Donna Karan Crepe Back satin dress with matching hosiery and her most beloved Christian Louboutin patent leather platform pumps and Michael Kors handbag. Pairing this with her newly acquired David Yurman diamond and sterling silver circle earrings, she admired herself in the mirror just before heading down to meet her limousine for the ride over. Maggie had a slight

uncertainty as to why Mace had asked her out to discuss

how she wanted Donald Roy delivered. Even so, she

wasn't about to allow that slight nagging feeling to keep

her from enjoying an even rarer night out.

It was ten minutes before eight when Mace

arrived at Franco's, handed the valet his keys, and

watched as he drove off in Mace's baby. Maggie arrived

moments later, looking stunning, and from the way he

stared at her, she knew what he was thinking. They met

in the lobby and went up to the hostess who ushered

them to the table. Stefano, the server, suggested they

each try their special Bellini cocktail when he arrived with

the menus. The special of the night was Lobster Fra

Diavolo for two and they added a bottle of Nicolas

Fuillatte Rose Champagne to the meal. As they sipped the

drinks, Mace couldn't take his eyes off of Maggie who

smiled coyly and asked, "Is something on your mind, Mace?" "   "Maggie, I just have to tell you how absolutely beautiful you look tonight, and I'm honored to be sitting here with you," he said with a smile.

She almost blushed as she thanked him and replied, "Well, you're looking pretty fantastic yourself, my friend. I don't recall ever seeing you wear that tuxedo before tonight. It really fits you quite well. It wouldn't hurt you to dress like this more often Mace."

The meal was scrumptious, and the champagne and company almost distracted him from the real reason they were there. Maggie had been such a good friend, and Mace genuinely missed being around her the past thirteen months. It was hard for him to fathom her involvement in such a cold-blooded affair, but if his years of experience had taught him anything at all, it was that evidence didn't lie.

Tomorrow was coming like a freight train rolling down the tracks, and he would be forced to deliver an innocent man back into the Las Vegas legal system. Without giving away his true motive, Mace asked her if she believed it was possible for Donald Roy Perkins to receive a fair trial. She indicated that the jury and lawyers were charged with that responsibility. Her job was simply to oversee the proceedings and insure that the legal protocols were followed. Tiramisu arrived and they both dove in with spoons. The rich coffee flavored dessert was the perfect pairing for the lobster.

The night had flown by and it was time to bid his friend a fond farewell and good night. They hugged,

Mace gently kissed her cheek, and then she climbed into her limousine while he awaited the return of his car by the valet. Mace went straight home and undressed before landing exhausted in his bed.

The water from his morning shower had created a fog over the mirror. Mace used a towel in a circular motion until he could see his face, and then ran his hand over a stubbly chin. A look of anticipation and concern filled his eyes. The radio disc jockey gave the time as 8:19, and Mace hoped Donald Roy was readying himself for the upcoming events of the day. They both came to the conclusion last night that if he spent even one night in jail, he probably wouldn't survive since he had gone against everything he had been instructed to do. If the knife which bore his fingerprints was presented, his fate would be sealed regardless of his claims of innocence. This fact had caused Mace to attempt a desperate play to keep

Donald Roy from jail and certain death. With this thought at the forefront of his mind, he prayed it didn't blow up in his face. This crazy idea could cost Mace his career if it backfired, but he had to give it a try; his conscience simply wouldn't have it any other way.

The Saturn Sky pulled up outside of Glen's place, Mace honked the horn, and waited for Donald Roy to present himself. He and Glen stepped outside, and Mace felt a lump begin to grow in his throat. The passenger door swung open, and Donald Roy slipped into the seat and buckled in. "Good morning, Mace," he said.

"Good morning, guys," Mace replied. Glen made his way around to the driver's door and leaned in close to ask if Mace was sure he wanted to do this. Feigning more confidence than he really felt, he looked up at Glen and said, "C'mon, pal, you know I'd never do anything this risky if I didn't have a backup plan." Mace gave Glen his best smile, winked, and punched his shoulder before putting the car in reverse. "Trust me," Mace told him. "It'll all work itself out. You'll see."

The courtroom was empty when Donald Roy and Mace entered. This allowed them to go over the plan one more time. Donald assured Mace he knew his part and had full faith that justice would prevail. Even so Mace said, "Any deviation could cause suspicion to arise and place your life in immediate jeopardy." Maggie came in after several minutes had passed to announce that her bailiff had car trouble and was running a little late. She asked if Mace could stick around and wait before leaving Donald Roy in only her custody. He told her he needed to call Bonnie first because he didn't know what she had on his agenda for the day but that it shouldn't be a problem. Maggie nodded agreement. Mace cuffed Donald Roy to a chair back, picked up the iPhone, and since he couldn't

get a signal he headed to the foyer.

Silence filled the courtroom until Donald Roy

began to speak to Judge Winston. "I'm truly sorry that I

ran thirteen months ago instead of appearing here before

you, your Honor," Donald said. "Mace assures me after

the talk you two had last night, you're open to believing

my innocence, too. You don't know how hard it was to

see the bodies of my wife and daughter bloodied and

killed while I was restrained, totally unable to help them.

To know that everything important in your life had just

been taken from you, almost like you had nothing left to

live for. Then to be framed for the heinous act and forced

to evade the best skip tracer in the world while you lived

a meager existence almost convinced me to commit

suicide. Sometimes I awake in a cold sweat after having

had a horrible nightmare about the whole incident."

"Shut your mouth!" Maggie screamed. "I've heard enough of your sob story. What makes you think I care if you're innocent or guilty. You've been misinformed if Mace told you I believed that you are being railroaded. If I had it my way, every last one of you murdering scum would suffer for your crimes the same method that you chose for your victims. Do you have any idea how many times I've had to sit here in this chair behind this bench and watch lawyers screw up? IT SICKENS MY STOMACH TO THE POINT OF NAUSEA! They fail to follow the rules or prove their cases and allow the dregs of society to walk out scot-free. Well, not this time, mister. YOU'RE GOING TO PAY FOR WHAT YOU'VE DONE1! I GUARANTEE IT!"

Mace returned as Maggie was screaming the last two sentences. Donald's eyes were as big as saucers, and he glared at Mace when he got close. He said, "You lied to me, Mace! How could you? I trusted you, and you played me like a piano. You led me here knowing full well that Judge Winston never told you she believed my accusation was false."

"Hey, man," Mace said, "I've got a reputation to protect. If my telling you a little white lie got you here with minimal worry of you escaping again, I'd say it was worth it. Besides you can hate me all you want while you're doing your time in prison," he finished.

Dejectedly Donald Roy sat down, hung his head, and began to cry. Knowing he was a broken man, Mace decided to release him from the constraints of the handcuffs. Mace felt that Donald should enjoy the benefit of being a free man until he was taken into custody when the bailiff arrived.

Maggie motioned Mace to come over to where she was seated, and he walked up to the witness stand. Apparently this was the moment Donald Roy had been waiting for because he jumped over the railing and began to run for the exit. Mace drew his trusty Glock22 from its holster and yelled, "Stop or I'll shoot!" He lowered the sight onto his back and Donald turned to face him. Donald said, "I ain't going to prison, Mace, so you might as well shoot me," and he turned back towards the door. Two steps later, Mace's instincts took over, and he felt the familiar recoil coursing through his hand as Donald dropped to the floor and smoke rose from the barrel of the pistol.

The sound reverberated in the empty room causing Maggie to cover her ears. In a flash Mace had reached the crumpled body of Donald Roy Perkins as he lay in a pool of blood just feet from the exit he had used for his escape a little more than a year ago. Mace placed his fingers on Donald's carotid artery and felt no pulse; he had killed Donald Roy with three shots through the back center mass around his heart and reported the same to Maggie.

Suddenly there was a rage in Maggie's eyes Mace had never witnessed before. She screamed "Mace, why did you kill him? Couldn't you have shot him in the leg or something? He should have suffered for what he's done. I'm sick and tired of people like him walking on the feelings of others and ruining their lives. They crush the hopes and dreams of people they so called love and pay no heed to the ramifications of their actions. Well, I had made certain that wasn't going to happen this time, but now you've ruined it."

Grabbing her shoulders and staring into her eyes, Mace asked, "What are you talking about, Maggie?"

"Do you have any idea how much this cost me to set up, Mace? How many favors I had to call in and the deals I had to make with the vilest of humanity? I've had to throw my morals out the window, spend a large portion of my savings, risk my entire career and everything I stand for to fulfill a promise I made to my best friend at her funeral."

Her confession stunned Mace, and he could hardly believe his ears. Mace asked what could have happened that would make her risk everything she'd worked for in her life. The story that followed sent shivers up his spine. She began by telling him about her goddaughter Rhonda Russell, the only child of her college roommate and best friend Rebecca Martin. She had returned home to Chicago after the break up with Donald Roy and fallen into a deep depression. All night binge drinking had become the only activity in which she would participate. One night after consuming too much alcohol,

she hit a tree while driving her mother's car to the store

to buy more booze and wound up paralyzed. Confined to

a wheelchair proved very taxing on Rebecca and her

grades suffered. Slowly, but surely, Rhonda sank deeper

and deeper into her shell and pulled her mother down,

also. Finally, exhausted from the needs of her daughter,

Rebecca was forced to drop out of law school and give up

on her dream of becoming a litigator.

Maggie continued with how she had tried

everything she knew including counseling and things

appeared to be getting better little by little. Then one day

watching television, Rhonda saw a feature on Donald Roy

and his new family, and those old emotions returned

bringing back destructive behaviors. About six years ago

now Maggie had received a call from Rebecca telling her

that Rhonda, overwhelmed by depression, had climbed

into a hot bath and slit her wrists. When she went to check on her daughter, she found her dead from the self-inflicted wounds. Immediately, she picked up the phone and called her best friend Maggie, who took the first flight out to comfort her through the grieving process. On the third day of her visit, Rebecca came into the living room with tears streaming down her cheeks, shook her head, shrugged her shoulders, and whispered, "I'm sorry." After which she calmly pulled a handgun from her housecoat and blew her head off. The note that was left behind said she couldn't go on without her daughter and she regretted ever suggesting the University of Florida to Rhonda. The final line said she trusted Maggie would take care of things in whatever manner she saw fit.

It was after reading that note and experiencing the traumatic events of the visit that she had hatched the plan to find Donald Roy and do whatever it took to make him suffer for the loss he had caused her and the pain inflicted on her friend and daughter. As the story poured out of Maggie, the color of her face gradually returned to its normal shade, and she wilted like a flower in the scorching summer heat. The metamorphosis was something to behold. Black streaks from her tears marred Maggie's otherwise perfect makeup and made her appear clownish. Mace holstered his pistol and walked over to the prosecutor's table where she had put her head into her hands. Her wrath now dissipated she became fully aware of what she had done. The realization of what she had caused Mace to do began to set in. She raised her head and began to apologize for making him kill Donald Roy Perkins. The sobs were so strong they shook her body uncontrollably. It was like seeing the destruction uncovered as floodwaters recede and expose the total damage hidden underneath.

"Maggie," Mace asked, "are those your fingerprints are on the money we found in the envelopes that were sent to Darla? Were you supplying her and others with the locations of my team and me? Please help me understand why Glen and Karla had to be beaten and Mark nearly stabbed to death." She replied that once she had given the latest information to her henchmen, they handled the details on their own. She hadn't realized the methods they'd used to guarantee the necessary results had jeopardized anyone except Donald Roy. The instructions she'd given were to get him back to Las Vegas so he could be found guilty and then be made to suffer as much as possible in prison. She was planning to put in with criminals she had sentenced and have them beat and control and otherwise cause him a miserable existence.

Mace was dumbfounded and stared at her in disbelief when she said, "That's it, Mace. That's the whole sordid story." Mace told her she would have to be placed under arrest and stand trial for her involvement in this criminal activity. She said, "I don't think so, Mace. It's your word against mine, and I'll just deny it. You haven't any proof, my friend." Mace replied, "That's not quite true, Maggie. I've got a recording of your confession. Right, Donald Roy?"

"Yes, we do, Mace," Donald replied.

A look of shock came over Maggie's face as the blood stained body at the exit door arose and walked over to the table. "But I, I saw you shoot him...how can he be alive?" she stated in disbelief.

"Oh, I had loaded my gun with blanks, and we staged that little escape scene for your benefit," Mace replied. "I suspected you had something to do with this, but I had no idea you were the mastermind behind it. The bailiff is waiting outside, along with several of Las Vegas' finest to take you away. You need some help, Maggie," Mace said, "and now you'll get it."

As the police handcuffed Maggie and began to take her away she said, "I can't believe you set me up like this, Mace."

He replied, "Darlin', you did this to yourself when you took matters into your own hands. I'll stop in to see you from time to time. You can count on that. You are the absolute last person I would have ever imagined being capable of something so heartless, Maggie Winston."

Donald Roy stopped Mace, looked at her, and said, "I'm so very sorry that Rhonda and Rebecca both killed themselves, Judge Winston. Rhonda and I had a great thing going for a while, but then one day she just gave me an ultimatum. She said I either had to choose college or her. My parents had scrimped and saved many years trying to pay for my education. I couldn't just drop out and get married like she demanded. I promised them both I'd serve the USA and make them proud of me. The next day Rhonda was gone, and all I could do was rededicate myself to my schoolwork and the Army. Until now, I've wondered what happened to her, but I had no idea she was deceased.

"Though I can understand the pain you've been through and can even sympathize to some degree, my wife and daughter were innocent and had nothing to do with any of this," Donald said. "The gruesome way they were killed reminded me of some of the carnage from war zones I've seen. It somehow gets inside your mind and eats away at your very soul, and no one should ever have to experience that, especially with their five-year-old child. I will NEVER forget the anguish you've caused or the lives you've ruined, but as a Christian man, I pray in time I will be able to forgive you."

News of Maggie's arrest spread quickly through legal circles, and it wasn't long before Joshua was ringing Mace's cell phone. "Mace, can you confirm for me that Judge Winston was arrested for accessory to murder today? "He asked.

"Yes, I can," Mace answered. "She confessed to the whole gruesome plot regarding the murder of Donald Roy Perkins' wife and daughter. The Las Vegas police have her in custody awaiting her arraignment hearing to be held in the Lloyd D. George Federal Courthouse. Don't worry though, Joshua," Mace said. "I'm sure old man Caston will still make you a partner if that's what you're worried about."

With a half-hearted laugh, unsure if Mace was serious or just chiding him a little, Joshua replied, "Don't you worry either, man. My offer to treat you and your team to a night on the town still stands even though you proved Donald Roy innocent.

"Touché, Joshua, touché," Mace sighed.

They agreed to meet the next week at Wolfgang Puck's Bar and Grill on Wednesday night around six. The restaurant offered glasses and bottles of wine for half off the regular price then, and that's all Joshua drank. A selection of hand-crafted cocktails, plus domestic and imported beers were available, along with a choice cut of steak for a reasonable price. They ate and drank until they'd all had their fill. Joshua excused himself first saying now that this case had finally ended he was going to see Dawn and attempt to repair their broken relationship. Karla and Glen departed next claiming it was time for some much needed sleep. Donald Roy and Mace toasted

his innocence one last time with a shot of Bushmill 1608

Anniversary Edition whiskey. Lowering their glasses to

the table they locked eyes for just a second. In that sliver

of time, an unspoken respect and appreciation passed

between two men both hardened by service to their

country. They nodded their heads and Donald Roy softly

spoke.

"Mace, words can't express my thanks and

gratitude for all that you've done for me. Now that this is

over, I can return to my home state of Florida and finally

mourn my wife and daughter. I've kept it all locked up

and buried deep down inside since the night it occurred.

My rage kept me warm on those cold, lonely nights, but

it's time I learn to let it go and move on. I've already been

in touch with my folks, and they're anxiously waiting to

see me again. Should you ever find yourself in a tight

spot and need a friend, all you need to do is send up the SOS. I'll be there man. You can count on me."

Mace shook Donald Roy's hand as he was preparing to get in the Saturn Sky. Mace lowered the top, cranked the volume up on the radio, buckled in and then he headed for the airport. There was a beach somewhere calling his name, and he was going to answer it before somebody put him back to work. Maybe he'd take in the sights of Bora Bora, or Cancun or perhaps Tahiti. He'd allow the airline schedules to decide for him. He'd earned this vacation, and he was taking it. Warm sunshine, cool drinks, white sands, pounding surf and scantily clad women...all waited for his enjoyment. He planned to lay on a chaise lounge chair beneath a beach umbrella with no intention of thinking of work or stress or anything except recharging his batteries and allowing himself the fantasy of a life with Linda. "Damn right! My life is good!" he roared as he rolled on through traffic headed

for McCarran International Airport.

Made in the USA
San Bernardino, CA
18 April 2016